KIYOSHI

and the

GRUMPY GHOST

Nik Forster

First published in 2018 on Amazon Kindle by Ex-L-Ence Publishing a division of Winghigh Limited, England.
www.ex-l-ence.com
This paperback edition published in 2018

Copyright © Nik Forster 2018

The right of Nik Forster to be identified as the author of this work has been asserted by him in accordance with sections 77 and 78 of the Copyright Designs and Patents Act 1988.

All rights reserved. No part of this publication may be reproduced, stored in a retrieval system, or transmitted, in any form or by any means, electronic, mechanical, photocopying, recording or otherwise, without the prior permission of the copyright owner.

This book is a work of fiction and any resemblance between the characters in this work and any persons, living or dead, is purely coincidental. Nothing is intended or should be interpreted as representing or expressing the views and policies of any department or agency of any government, Church, or other body.

All trademarks used are the property of their respective owners. All trademarks are recognised.

Cover Design Copyright © Karen Lundin 2018

ISBN 978-1-6446-7901-2

Printed and bound by Ingram Spark

Dedicated to my father Richard Forster for his encouragement. Also with thanks to Karen Lundin for her invaluable help.

ALSO BY NIK FORSTER

Salo: Canine Outlaw

Karateka

Blazer: The Story of a Fighting Dog

PREFACE

I had the good fortune to live three years in Japan, in which time I grew to know many of the customs and the lifestyle of the Japanese people. To my shame I never mastered the language except the basics.

My flat was a few stations away from Ikebukuro in Tokyo but I've set the location of this story in a fictitious coastal village, based on a visit to Shikine-jima, one of the seven islands off Tokyo.

The Japanese enjoy ghost stories, either horror or traditional folk lore; inspired by this, I've written it more as a humorous take on the supernatural, involving a Japanese teacher of English and a deceased ancient mariner seeking eternal peace.

I can only hope this book might encourage others to visit this fascinating country, and those that have, to rekindle fond memories.

CHAPTER 1

A spectre calls

Kiyoshi took a detour along the river back toward the park where Bartholomew's skeleton had been discovered. He ignored the weather, wrapped in his thoughts he tried to formulate in his mind the best course of action; he sat down on a bench. Any passer-by would assume that the forlorn character seated alone in the middle of the park was homeless or derelict, or even on the verge of suicide.

'How did I get into this mess?' he mumbled. His mind drifted back to where it all started.

It was a cold January night; he remembered glancing at the clock, it was a minute to midnight. The sumo wrestling highlights of the day had finished moments earlier and bed seemed an ideal choice. He heard his mother's snores from upstairs almost the same volume as the roar of the wind and withdrew his legs from beneath the electrically heated table he shared with Kuro their cat.

His balding head reflected the light from a nearby lamp as he leant down and pulled the plug on his companion's source of comfort.

Kiyoshi was forty-two years old, a teacher at the local school. He had been coerced by the headmaster to take on the task of English tutor although equipped with sparse knowledge of the subject.

He lived in a small coastal village five hours drive from Tokyo, and shared with his mother a two-bedroom house that had been in the family for many years.

Kiyoshi and the Grumpy Ghost

Kiyoshi Hirota's life was unexciting, mundane a more appropriate description demonstrated by his behaviour on school holidays when he would spend most of his time either asleep or swilling beer at the izakaya, the local "pub" come eating house.

He had fallen in love with Kaoru Endo, a young woman who lived in the same village but due to his lack of confidence in his ability to woo the fair sex, his ardour remained unrequited. There was another "problem", Kaoru was of Korean descent and although his mother never said, he knew she would not approve.

Mrs. Hirota was well into her seventies but retained a remarkable amount of youthful vigour and constantly reminded Kiyoshi that he was the last male in the family to carry on the Hirota name.

Kiyoshi was aware of the genetic burden he carried in his loins but refused to accommodate his mother when she arranged several introductions to various eligible females from "good families". He had gone along with her in so far as he agreed to meet the prospective brides but declined to show further enthusiasm for any long-term commitment. At the back of his mind was sweet Kaoru, but fear of her rejection, was the major stumbling block to his happiness.

He stood up, stretched and yawned. The cat, from under the table, rotated its left ear and then returned it to its previous position. A loud knock on the front door caused both of his feline ears to face in the direction of the sound. It was insufficient motivation to stir the creature but evoked in Kiyoshi a grunt of disbelief that anyone would call at this time. He stood undecided; should he ignore it? The knock was repeated this time louder. It was unusual but his curiosity got the better of him.

"Who the hell is it?" he muttered to himself.

A cold gust of air lashed his face as he opened the door but the shock of the icy blast diminished into total insignificance by the sight that beheld him.

Framed in the doorway was a scruffy Gaijin, a foreigner, with long unkempt hair, dirty clothes and tangled beard. Kiyoshi in a

A spectre calls

state of shock was able to discern movement of the concealed lips through the mass of hirsute growth. He felt his bowels contract and with a supreme effort of will managed to avoid total evacuation of his earlier meal. His emotional state fluctuated from panic, to terror, and back to panic.

Although a teacher of English he regarded foreigners as odd, their behaviour and customs strange and their attitude towards Japanese people generally superior, sometimes prone to arrogance.

He avoided any kind of contact where possible and had once had the misfortune to be called upon to give directions to a large American who had stupidly, as Kiyoshi thought, gotten himself lost.

Perhaps one reason he disliked social intercourse with native English speakers was that it demonstrated how poor his command of the language was; like a lot of Japanese students of English, his written grammar was a lot better than many for whom it is their native tongue, but conversationally left a lot to be desired.

Kiyoshi, with a supreme effort of will stammered out the words, 'What do you want?'

The person spoke; his voice boomed out and drowned the weakly pitched question from Kiyoshi. The stranger addressed him in English.

'I wish to converse with you on a matter of great importance,' the voice requested.

'Huh?' replied Kiyoshi his own voice in falsetto.

The stranger repeated his question. Kiyoshi gaped and echoed his previous comment, 'Huh?'

'Prithee may I enter your abode good sir? May I step in?'

Kiyoshi's mind raced, he understood what was meant by "step in" and closed the door almost shut to reveal as little of his features.

Kiyoshi and the Grumpy Ghost

'Er you er go see Masada San, er ano, er he have hotel he look after, he live two doors left.'

Kiyoshi didn't wait for the Gaijin's reply but slammed the door as hard as he could in the man's face. He stood and listened for any movement.

The wind made it impossible for him to discern anything of lesser volume. His heart pounded and his intake of breath rapid as he strained his ears for any sound other than the north wind. He had heard about foreigners who attacked people asleep in their beds, none were to be trusted.

He remained against the door for two or three minutes; he was about to return to the living room to switch off the light, convinced that even at this moment the hairy savage had positioned himself on the doorstep of Mr. Masada, a man he didn't have a great deal of time for, and could now have the problem of how to deal with such an intrusion, when he heard a screech from Kuro, the obese feline, the apple of his mother's eye, give vent to a scream that sent a shiver down Kiyoshi's spine and once again tested his bowel control. He raced into the room and was met by the cat, its body even more rotund by erect follicles and fluffed up tail, as it made an undignified exit.

He heard the animal's claws rake the tatami, then a pause, and then a dull thud that communicated the pussy's head had come into contact with the cat door, a somewhat non-Japanese device, which had unfortunately been closed by Mrs. Hirota before she retired for the night. Silence. Kiyoshi entered the room and despite another supreme effort on his part, evacuated his bowels.

The sight that stimulated this lapse of control was that of the Gaijin in the middle of the room casually stroking his beard. Mother Nature has some strange ways in which she conducts her affairs, Kiyoshi's response perhaps a good example. Its function practical if faced by some evil predator wishing to satisfy its hunger pangs; it gets rid of unnecessary weight and enables more rapid movement of retreat, or whatever. It may also create rather an unpleasant odour to distract the attention of the attacker. Unfortunately, in Kiyoshi's case it served no other purpose but to

A spectre calls

soil his underpants and perhaps because of the loss of ballast, caused him to sink to the floor slower than he would have done a few moments earlier.

The stranger looked at the fallen man and shook his head.

'A brave heart indeed,' he muttered as he moved to the other side of the room; he waited.

Kiyoshi remained where he fell, eventually to stir and rise on unsteady feet. He remembered the cause of his sudden lapse of consciousness and turned to face the man who stood quietly in the corner.

'Feeling better are we?' the stranger asked.

Kiyoshi's mouth was dry and he felt the sensation of naked fear within him.

'Go away, you go now, this my house. I call police.'

'Please control yourself. I have no desire to harm you; I wish only to enlist your aid.'

'What do you want?' Kiyoshi repeated slowly, as he tried to think how to handle the situation, still convinced that he and his mother would be found in the morning with their throats cut and their possessions stolen.

'Listen to me, just listen.' The stranger leaned toward Kiyoshi and mouthed the words, 'Do you understand? Listen. L-I-S-T-E-N.'

Kiyoshi nodded but couldn't find the required vocal energy to make a sound.

The stranger drew himself up to his full height and began.

'What I am about to tell you will no doubt cause you to feel perhaps a little apprehensive of me?'

This was an unnecessary statement for Kiyoshi could not have been more apprehensive if he'd tried.

The stranger continued, 'I am, and I know that you will find this difficult to believe, a ghost, a spirit, a wandering soul seeking

Kiyoshi and the Grumpy Ghost

eternal rest from this accursed dimension that I once inhabited, but now have the misfortune to share with those of a more substantial composition.'

Kiyoshi listened to the stranger but managed to decipher about a third of the man's words. His comprehension was better than his conversational ability but still left a lot to be desired. He was puzzled as to how the Gaijin got into his front room, he could only assume that he'd entered from the back whilst he waited at the front. He understood the word ghost but failed to register its implication in respect to the situation he now experienced; he put it down to the man being a complete madman which added to the conviction of his and his mother's imminent demise.

He wasn't the bravest of souls as demonstrated by his sludgy underwear, but he began to formulate a plan. Next to the lamp was an umbrella placed there by himself upon his return from the pub. The man would occasionally turn his back on Kiyoshi, pace about the room then spin around to emphasise a point, or check that he was still conscious.

Kiyoshi feigned concentration and waited for the right moment. The man turned away and Kiyoshi with one swift movement lunged at the umbrella, grabbed hold of the lower part, swung it in an arc and brought the handle down with all the force he could muster on the stranger's head.

Kiyoshi prepared himself for the impact of the instrument against the skull of the intruder.

Instead of the dull thud of struck bone there was just the swish of the umbrella's fabric as it sliced through the air followed by a crack as the metal handle made contact with the floor.

The spirit turned in time to see the figure of Kiyoshi in the final stage of collapse.

He shrugged, gave a sigh of resignation and regarded the prostrate middle-aged schoolteacher flat out on the floor.

Minutes later Kiyoshi regained his senses, sat up and shook his head as if he tried to dislodge the events of the most recent past. The discomfort of the lower half of his anatomy and the unmistakable shape of the hairy foreigner large as life in the sanctuary of his living room, reassured him that no matter how many times he shook his head it would change nothing.

'Look, pray just sit there and listen, it is less distance to fall. As I was saying I am a ghost which no doubt you believe as demonstrated by your departure from your senses after that futile attempt to strike me from behind with that instrument; I am in need of your assistance, I need your help. Do you understand? I need your help. It would be an excellent and comforting consolation for me.'

The ghost's visage loomed uncomfortably close to Kiyoshi's face. The sight of several nose hairs protruding from the spook's nostrils presented themselves; Kiyoshi although in a state of shock wondered why Gaijin seem to have hairs grow out of wherever there is an orifice. Kiyoshi nodded and gaped in disbelief.

'Good, let me explain, I am, or rather was, an English naval captain, we were at war with the Dutch, and I was picked up by an enemy vessel off the coast of China after my ship was sunk. I was on a return trip to England after trading with Chinese and learned later that the Captain and crew of my captors had deserted the field of battle and fled.

As a prisoner I had no choice; I was forced to accompany this bunch of swarthy scum on a trip to the east where they would pick up victuals from this Island of your birth place, a venture that I was somewhat loathe to undertake. The crew were indeed an assortment of cutthroats and villains. As with most soulless individuals there is scant honour; there was a mutiny on board, the Captain tossed over the side and those not involved in the plot, murdered; I was considered a navigator and so spared, or so I thought.

Mother Nature had other plans and when we were off the coast of this God forsaken country a storm of such proportion blew up that the ship was wrecked and all hands, save myself and three seamen perished. The remains of our vessel were hurled against rocks and diminished to a tattered hulk of small worth, and there we resided until the storm abated. How the mutineers intended to leave the Island in the future I had no idea.

As many goods and valuables we could carry were transported from the hulk in the time the tide would allow, the vessel's total break up was imminent. We had as yet encountered no sign of human life and were of the mind that the place was uninhabited.

The Dutch mutineers at all times kept close regard as to my actions whilst my mind constantly thought of escape from this trio of cutthroats.

I was ordered to carry a box of treasure and precede the men to a favourable spot for its internment. A map was drawn of the location; I was instructed to dig a hole and gave thought as to why they should wish to intern their spoils rather than use it for their own purpose, and entertained an inclination that the men had hatched some scheme; but no idea as to the extent of their distaste of my person.

When the task was complete I was struck from behind by one of the pirates who wielded a somewhat more lethal object than the article you employed. My composition was then, good sir, a deal more resistant to the transit of objects and I crossed the line into a different sphere of existence. My body was dragged and thrown into a crevice in the earth. In which I may add I have been confined for these last few centuries.

This brings me to the need of my visit. For my soul to find eternal solace I must be buried according to the beliefs that I have lived by, as a God fearing Christian, and it falls to you my good sir to provide the remnants of my mortal coil a burial that befits a sea captain; at sea with a small service and a recital of chosen words from the good book. Can I depend on you, sir, to fulfil this task or do I ask too much?

Oh, my name is Bartholomew, Bartholomew James Christian Walker at your service sir.'

The spectre inclined his upper body in a gesture of respect to the open-mouthed Japanese man on the floor. Kiyoshi had listened as best he could. The foreigner, although he spoke slowly, used

A spectre calls

many words that were totally alien to Kiyoshi and to concentrate on what the man was saying as well as wrestle mentally with his own self-control was beyond him. He had managed to discern that the shape in front of him purported to be of another dimension and the ease at which his umbrella had passed through the apparition confirmed that there was an element of truth in this. He also understood that the "whatever" wanted his assistance for some reason. The rest of Bartholomew's conversation had sailed like the mariner's ship over his head and lost to the more immediate thought as to whether he had experienced what happened or was involved in some kind of nightmare?

Bartholomew waited for a response.

'Well, will you grant me your assistance sir?'

Kiyoshi's mind raced, he didn't want to upset the intruder and yet he hadn't understood in total what the ghost had waffled on about for the last few minutes.

'Er yes er I help.' He thought it best to appease the apparition, play along in order to facilitate his departure as expediently as possible; still convinced that he and his mother were in danger of imminent murder.

'What do you want me do?' Kiyoshi enquired.

Bartholomew made his way over to Kiyoshi. As he approached there was a distinct musky odour as well as the aroma from his own earlier indiscretion; he tried to recall where he had smelled it before, the former not the latter.

'I need writing materials,' Bartholomew stated in a manner that befitted a ship's captain. Kiyoshi looked bewildered.

'Writing materials, parchment, and a quill.'

Bartholomew mimed the act as if to write.

'Oh, and something to write upon.'

Kiyoshi's mental faculties began to grasp Bartholomew's request.

'Souka, pen, paper.'

Kiyoshi and the Grumpy Ghost

He struggled to his feet very much aware of his previous lapse of control and the discomfort it now caused, plus the rather unpleasant smell that wafted his way when he raised himself. His main concern at this particular moment was survival; all thoughts to regain more comfortable attire of secondary importance. The ghost seemed unaware of Kiyoshi's condition, or if he knew, gave no indication of such knowledge.

Whilst Kiyoshi hunted around the room for a pencil he kept one eye on the image of the Gaijin, but gave the impression his attention was elsewhere. The shape of his mother appeared in the doorway; bleary eyed, dishevelled hair and dour countenance. She glared at her son as he searched in the drawer.

'What are you looking for?' she boomed with a voice equally as formidable as Bartholomew's. Kiyoshi froze and no doubt would have repeated the same procedure as before when startled, had it not been for the fact that he recognised his mother's voice before the adrenalin had time to work. He looked at her; his mother looked back at him, Kiyoshi looked at Bartholomew.

'Well, what are you doing and what's that smell?'

Kiyoshi's mouth fell open. He turned slowly to Bartholomew and then back to his mother in disbelief.

'A Gaijin, a bloody great Gaijin,' he shouted.

His mother emulated her son's previous expression, not because she beheld the sight of Bartholomew, but because her son had bellowed at her for no apparent reason and called her a bloody great Gaijin.

'There... There, look can't you see him?' Kiyoshi pointed and emphasised the gesture with a thrust of his finger within an inch of Bartholomew's nose. His mother shook her head slowly.

'If you're trying to tell the good lady that there is someone else in the room other than you or her, save yourself the trouble. She cannot see me.'

Bartholomew opened his mouth wide and mouthed the words slowly.

A spectre calls

'She cannot see me, only you can see and hear me.'

Kiyoshi addressed his mother.

'You really can't see him. You can't see this man?'

'What on earth are you talking about? And where's Kuro?'

Kiyoshi rushed over to his mother, place his hands on her shoulders, and turned her toward Bartholomew.

'Mother please don't joke with me, are you seriously telling me that you cannot see anything in front of you?'

'Yes, I can see a picture of your father and a wall and...'

'I'm not talking about walls and pictures. I'm talking about him, him that Gaijin in the middle of the room. He has a beard and scruffy clothes and there is a musty smell, can't you smell it?'

His mother looked around the room and then back at her son. She shook her head.

'I can't see anybody and the only thing I can smell is you, it's disgusting, now stop making all this noise and get to bed, and make sure you have a shower before you do.'

She turned on her heel, muttered something about alcohol and departed; she called out the name of the cat as she left.

Kiyoshi gaped at Bartholomew.

'She no can see you, I am losing brain, I am go mad.'

'You are not mad good sir, I am as real as you only I am composed of how shall I say, material at the higher end of the physical plane, whilst you are still in the very raw stages of physical manifestation.'

'I no understand you, you talk strange English.'

'Never mind that, the point is that I am real, I am here, you are there, and I need your help, please fetch the parchment and quill.'

Kiyoshi and the Grumpy Ghost

Kiyoshi stared at the floor and pinched himself on the side of the face; yes, he was awake. The sensation of fear had subsided and although ill at ease with his present situation, he was able to move his body without the tremble in his limbs and the contraction of his bowels. He continued his search; a few moments later he produced the required articles. His mother returned with the cat draped over her left shoulder conscious after its encounter with the door.

'What happened to Kuro chan he seems very sleepy?'

'I think he must have seen the Gaijin,' Kiyoshi answered.

Mrs Hirota shook her head and left the room in time to prevent a repeat performance of Kuro's face against the closed door routine; the animal had begun to focus its vision into a somewhat clearer perspective and Bartholomew's shape was in the direct line of sight. Fortunately, the cat's brain was not able to decipher the material presented quickly enough to evoke a response and its glazed eyes treated to a rapid change of scenery.

Bartholomew gestured to Kiyoshi to give him the paper and pencil; Kiyoshi hesitated, he stretched out his arm; a cold chill ran through his hand and down his spine to send a shiver through his being. Bartholomew took the objects with a quick acknowledgment of thanks and began to draw a map.

Kiyoshi was still in a mild state of shock from his contact with a hand from another dimension and struggled again to exercise control over his limbs.

Bartholomew's voice brought his attention back to the needs of his uninvited guest.

'Now see here, this is where my remains are located, this is the very spot.'

Kiyoshi nodded and looked at the lines roughly drawn on the paper.

'Good,' he murmured, "remains" he was not clear on what the spectre had in mind but thought it best to humour the apparition as much as possible.

A spectre calls

Bartholomew turned to him, his face distorted with an expression of frustration.

'Sir you are a complete and utter buffoon, you have no idea what I am talking about have you?'

Kiyoshi nodded and gave a nervous smile as Bartholomew's mood changed.

'For God's sake sir, please listen and pay attention to what I say. Here are my bones,' Bartholomew pointed to a spot on the map marked with a cross.

'Bones, do you understand? My body.' Bartholomew indicated his torso. 'Here,' he quickly drew the shape of a skeleton on the paper. 'Bones,' he repeated.

Kiyoshi regarded the illustration and understood his meaning.

'Bones,' Bartholomew reiterated. 'My bones are here what I want you to do is to dig them up, do you understand?'

Kiyoshi slowly registered what the hairy Gaijin wanted, again his mouth gaped open like a large fish about to devour a smaller member of its species.

'You want me to dig bones?'

'Yes, yes at last a glimmer of comprehension in the tiny brain,' Bartholomew exclaimed, the look of frustration giving way to an avuncular expression that radiated warmth and benevolence.

Kiyoshi didn't notice, he was too busy with the rearrangement of his own facial muscles into a look of incredulous disbelief.

'And what I do with bones when I dig?' he asked as he utilised his newly formed expression.

'You bury them at sea and say a few words.'

'Sea, what mean I have to take to sea?' he replied and thought that his nightmare had just taken on a new dimension of unpleasantness.

'If I am to find peace I must be interned in the briny, the wild and wasteful ocean, buried beneath the waves with a service that releases me from the bondage of this dimension, but there is a condition attached to my freedom. I have entered your realm for the first time in four hundred years. I have only three full moons to fulfil my quest, if I cannot be returned to the sea by then I shall be forced to wander the coast of your land for eternity never to find peace or release for my soul.'

Kiyoshi grasped forty percent of what Bartholomew had said, and realised that he was being asked to retrieve the skeleton and place it somewhere else, and, because he heard the word "sea", deduced that he was required to dispose of it in water. What moons had to do with anything hadn't quite sunk in. Bartholomew waved the map at Kiyoshi.

'My remains are here.' He pointed a ghostly finger at the map. Kiyoshi studied it for a few moments. He had no idea where the place was.

'Where is this place?' Kiyoshi enquired.

Bartholomew indicated a spot on the map.

'Here, here it is.'

'I can see drawing but where is place real life?'

'Don't you know?' Bartholomew enquired, 'how long have you lived in this village?'

'I born here but map has no familiar places for me, and I no mean to be rude, but not so good.'

Bartholomew regarded him for a moment then spoke.

'Where do you know in the village that has a stream and a temple of some kind? It must be close, within five furlongs.'

Kiyoshi had no idea what a furlong was and didn't ask but assumed that it was some form of measurement.

'There was temple but it destroyed by typhoon maybe twenty year ago and built again different place.'

'How long was it there before it was destroyed by the typhoon?'

A spectre calls

'Long time, many many year,' Kiyoshi answered and hoped that the apparition would just disappear.

'It must be the same one.' Bartholomew muttered to himself, 'and what about the stream?'

'You mean little river?'

'Yes river, stream, same thing.'

Bartholomew looked perplexed.

'On the morrow we shall go together and I will know for sure if my skeleton is there.'

Kiyoshi's mind had subsided from panic mode and he began to think clearer. He was under the impression that the spectre had requested his company the next morning for a walk.

The idea of a stroll along the road in the company of a person who had been dead for several decades was not exactly a prospect he looked forward to. He wondered why the ghost could not just whizz over there now and find out if it was the same place or not; and why he had not done that before he came to his house and literally scared the shit out of him? He also wanted to ask him what the hell he had done for the last few hundred years; if he had wandered around the coast for so long why hadn't he picked up even a little knowledge of Japanese?

Kiyoshi controlled his curiosity to avoid as much social intercourse with the unwanted intruder as possible, and if it meant that Bartholomew would vacate his premises if he kept his mouth shut, then he would do just that.

'I shall see you on the morrow good sir, pray tell me before I leave you to your slumber what is your name?'

'Kiyoshi,' he responded.

Bartholomew repeated the name.

'Fare thee well and I apologise if I gave thee fright, I wish you or the good lady no harm only your assistance. Goodnight.'

Kiyoshi and the Grumpy Ghost

Bartholomew faded away, with him went Kiyoshi's immediate concern for his safety and the musky smell that had pervaded his front room since the ghost's intrusion. He stared into space and contemplated the events of the past thirty minutes or so.

It was cold in the small room; the wind could be heard outside as if it searched for a way in to the confines of the house. Kiyoshi picked up the piece of paper and regarded the handwriting. His mind struggled to come to terms with what a few hours earlier he would have thought ridiculous and pure fantasy.

The room temperature began to intrude upon his senses, not to mention the discomfort of his earlier indiscretion; he waddled with short pigeon like steps toward the bathroom.

He turned on the shower and stood beneath the spray of water; what course of action should he take, should he report the events to some higher authority?

Why would they believe him any more than his mother? He did have the note but that was hardly proof it was written by a three or four hundred year old spook, and they would have to believe him, or at least half believe him to take the trouble to run tests? That's if there were any tests to provide evidence.

The warm water began to reassure him of one of the physical advantages of a more solid structure than that of a similar composition to his recent visitor; he turned his face toward the source of warmth and gratefully allowed the water to trickle down his forehead.

Kiyoshi ran his hands across his near bald head, rubbed his eyes and gave a long sigh that tailed off into a groan at the prospect of his liaison next morning.

Perhaps he wouldn't turn up, perhaps it wasn't real? Some alcohol induced hallucination; after all he did rather give it a bit of a nudge earlier, more than he usually did. Maybe his mother was right; perhaps he should give booze the elbow.

This thought reassured him, but only momentarily; he knew that what had taken place this evening had nothing to do with his intake of sake and whatever the explanation, there was more to come.

CHAPTER 2

Inconvenience

Kiyoshi spent a restless night and fell asleep as dawn's first rays of light penetrated his bedroom.

He was only allowed a few moments slumber, insufficient to experience the beneficial effects of rapid eye movement, before his mother stood over him and expounded the virtues of the cold January morning.

Kiyoshi groaned, his mind regurgitated the events prior to when he took to his bed.

'Has anyone called?' he enquired.

'Has anything, er, strange happened?'

His mother regarded her bleary eyed and unshaven son.

'Only your behaviour last night.'

She placed a cup of green tea by his bedside, drew back the blinds and invited more unwelcome light into Kiyoshi's room.

'Breakfast in a few minutes.' As she left, the cat passed her on its way in.

Kiyoshi's eyes focused on the rotund feline as it leapt onto his bed and purred loudly, its two front paws rhythmically pounded the eiderdown.

He reached out and stroked the cat's head; it butted against his hand and wiped feline saliva onto his wrist.

'You saw him didn't you Kuro, I'm not crazy am I?'

Inconvenience

For the cat the question posed no mental effort, all he heard was a series of sounds pitched at a level which excited no particular response and combined with the caress of fingers around the ears, indicated to the animal it had a good chance to fulfil his goal, to curl its corpulent body beneath the warmth of Kiyoshi's bed.

Kiyoshi on the other hand didn't expect a reply, but after the previous evenings experience, he would have been unsurprised to receive an answer.

As he vacated the comfort of his bed the cat immediately took up residence; Kiyoshi thought, not for the first time, that he should have been born a cat instead of a human being. His life was a constant struggle against enormous odds in the shape of hundreds of adolescent "monsters" who conspired to make his life as difficult as possible.

He caught the scent of breakfast; normally it would have stimulated his digestive juices, on this morning he had no appetite. His mind occupied with the arrival of Bartholomew; would he actually materialise as threatened?

He threw his clothes on, made his way down to breakfast and looked around in order to ascertain any indication of anything unworldly. His mother had set breakfast and was in the kitchen about to boil some water for more tea. Kiyoshi had ignored the first cup; he looked at the various dishes.

There was fish, the usual boiled rice with a raw egg, pickles and a small dish of various fruit. It did nothing to stimulate his taste buds. His mother returned with tea on a small tray; she remained silent, placed it on the table, knelt down, picked up a bowl, scooped some rice into it from the rice cooker, cracked an egg on top, and handed it to Kiyoshi who had joined her at the table. With eyes red from lack of sleep he stared blankly at the yolk of the egg, it reminded him of Kaoru's breast as it wobbled in the dish. The thought of the girl he yearned for caused him to forget about the prospect of his liaison with Bartholomew.

Kiyoshi and the Grumpy Ghost

His reverie was rudely interrupted by the faint smell of musk and the appearance of Bartholomew as large as life or perhaps death, next to him at the table.

Kiyoshi's bowels instantly contracted but he managed to avoid evacuation; his face turned ashen and the hair on his head became erect. His mother took a piece of fish from her bowl and placed it in her mouth; halfway through the process of mastication her jaws ceased their task and came to an abrupt halt; she had caught sight of the few follicles left on her son's shiny pate erect as though they had been blown by a sudden stiff breeze. Kiyoshi stared pale-faced into space.

'Good morning.' Bartholomew boomed.

Kiyoshi with a magnificent effort somehow overrode the emotion to scream with terror, stammered out a response.

'G G Good morning,' he replied.

'Eh?' his mother answered.

Kiyoshi turned to his mother and then to Bartholomew; his mouth agape at the sudden appearance of something he was sure did exist but hoped against all odds that it didn't. He again, faced his mother who showed no sign of awareness that a few feet away sat the figure of an unkempt ghost over four hundred years old. Or if she was aware, she kept pretty cool about it.

'Can you see anything... er... I mean unusual?'

His mother resumed her oral attention to the remnants of the fish, shook her head slowly and said nothing.

'I trust you slept well?' Bartholomew enquired.

'I sleep not so good.' Kiyoshi stated.

'Eh?' his mother answered.

Kiyoshi decided that if his mother could not see the dirty great ghost that sat in her breakfast then it would be futile to try to explain to her the image that he himself could see so clearly. A thought struck him.

Inconvenience

The cat, Kuro.

'Wait a minute.' Kiyoshi jumped up from the table. His mother stopped her mastication and watched as Kiyoshi, hair still erect, leapt up and raced upstairs in order to introduce Kuro to the ghost, in person.

Kuro could see the scruffy Gaijin for sure; his reaction would confirm that Bartholomew was not a hallucination.

The cat was fast asleep in a world of its own when the covers of the bed were thrown back and he was dragged backwards from his "nest." With outstretched claws in order to secure a foothold in the bedding, he endeavoured to slow down the process of removal, if not prevent it.

'Come here Kuro, I need you for a minute, a little demonstration.'

The "little demonstration," may have helped convince his mother that there was some truth in her son's story, but Bartholomew had followed Kiyoshi up the stairs, and appeared in the bedroom at the same time.

The cat, whilst resisting Kiyoshi's efforts to withdraw its corpulent body from beneath the eiderdown, happened to glance over his shoulder in order to register displeasure at such conduct; he was greeted by the sight of Bartholomew as he hovered next to the perpetrator of his discomfort. The creature transformed its fluffy rotund pussy body into a twelve-pound ball of fury, spat, growled then shot like a jet propelled fur coated missile from Kiyoshi's grasp, fled downstairs through the cat door, which this time was fortunately open, and into the garden. The terrified feline only stopped when it had gone several hundred yards from the house.

Kiyoshi knew why and felt the hairs on the back of his neck tingle.

'Something must have frightened it,' Bartholomew commented.

Kiyoshi said nothing; he thought many things but voiced none.

Kiyoshi and the Grumpy Ghost

'Are you ready to go then?' Bartholomew enquired in a casual manner as if he asked the family if they were organised for a Sunday picnic.

'Er, no I no dressed yet and no wash,' Kiyoshi stammered.

'Well hurry then good sir the sooner this task is complete the better for all I'm thinking.'

'Where we go?' Kiyoshi asked.

'To try and find the spot where I was savagely and brutally murdered.'

Kiyoshi was unfamiliar with the word brutal but had heard "murder" mentioned a few times from the television.

'I get dressed and am coming,' Kiyoshi announced; although the thought that he would have to spend time in the company of a ghost was the last thing he wanted.

A voice came from the doorway of his bedroom.

'Who are you talking to?' announced his mother.

'What was all that noise about, was that Kuro racing down the stairs?'

Kiyoshi and Bartholomew both looked at his mother as she stood arms folded and glared into the untidy confines of her son's room.

'I'm just practising my English, so maybe I will talk to myself for a while in English,' Kiyoshi explained.

'And yes it was the cat I think he may have wanted to go out in a hurry.'

He didn't even try to explain further and reconciled himself that he must handle this alone. He never usually confided his affairs to his mother; on the contrary he made every effort to conceal them from her, mostly without much success.

Mrs Hirota shook her head in disbelief.

'Have you been teasing him?'

Inconvenience

'No, if you really wish to know he saw a ghost.'

'The one you saw last night I presume,' his mother replied with a hint of sarcasm in her voice.

'Come downstairs and finish your breakfast before it gets too cold,' she commanded.

'I'll be down in a minute,' Kiyoshi mumbled.

'Is this lady your mother?' Bartholomew boomed.

Kiyoshi turned. She must have heard that surely?

'Yes,' replied Kiyoshi.

'What did you say?' his mother called from the stairs.

Kiyoshi rushed out onto the small landing,

'You heard it then?' he said excitedly.

'She only heard you,' Bartholomew responded guessing the question by Kiyoshi's actions and intonation.

'Heard what?' his mother replied.

Kiyoshi rubbed his eyes and brushed back one of the few long strands of hair on his head that had clung to existence whilst the majority had given up years ago.

'Nothing,' he said dejectedly.

'I will return when you are suitably attired.' Bartholomew faded from view.

Kiyoshi gave a low moan and went down to finish his breakfast.

An hour later found him seated in the living room, his overcoat and umbrella at the ready. His mother cleaned the mirror; she looked at the reflection of her son as he shifted uneasily in the chair.

'What are you waiting for? You look as though you're about to visit the dentist, and why have you got your coat on?'

'I have to leave soon.'

'Are you going drinking again?'

'No I'm er going out for a walk to get some fresh air,' Kiyoshi replied.

'Well then, you can pop into the convenience store and pick up some soy sauce.'

'I may not be going that way I will maybe walk near where the old temple used to be.'

'What's so interesting around that area?'

'How long was that temple there before it was relocated, and why did they move it?' Kiyoshi enquired whilst he mentally prepared himself for the reappearance of Bartholomew.

'Who knows, I think it was built a good few hundred years ago and then after the earthquake they moved it, but there had been rumours of strange sightings.'

Kiyoshi's interest was instantly aroused.

'What kind of strange sightings?'

'Oh a load of rubbish it was a story concocted by the council to sell some land on the other side of the village. So they put out rumours of spirits haunting the place.'

'But they may have been true.' Kiyoshi looked intently at his mother.

'Nonsense, I know Councillor Takashi and I wouldn't trust him any further than I trusted your father. He's still a schemer making millions of yen any way he can by using his position to wheel and deal.'

Kiyoshi was about to enquire further of his mother's knowledge of ghostly occurrences at the temple, when one took place in the middle of the living room.

'Ah Koshi you're ready I see for our journey.'

Kiyoshi although prepared had been caught off guard by the sudden arrival of Bartholomew. He recoiled and let out an involuntary gasp.

Inconvenience

His mother looked at him.

'What's the matter now?' she inquired.

Kiyoshi ignored his mother and turned towards Bartholomew.

'Please you show mother.'

Bartholomew shook his head,

'I'm sorry I can't do that.'

'Why not?' Kiyoshi replied.

'I must conserve my cosmic energy, I only have little time and a limited amount of energy and I don't want to waste it on impressing others.'

Kiyoshi's mother gazed at her son in the reflection of the mirror as he conversed in an animated manner in a foreign tongue.

She knew that foreigners gesticulated a lot whilst they conversed, so imagined that her son practised the unnecessary expressions and mannerisms that Gaijin were prone to employ. All the same it still looked odd and she began to think that her son could need some kind of help if he continued in this manner.

She finished the mirror and moved on to the television screen.

'You should get a wife and have some children and then you'd have things to think about other than yourself.'

Kiyoshi had heard the same lines over and over and knew it was time to depart before the onset of another lecture.

'Yes mother.' He rose from the chair, walked towards the front door and slipped into his outdoor shoes.

'I won't be long and if I go near the convenience store I'll buy some soy sauce.'

Kiyoshi said goodbye and closed the door. In his haste to depart he had omitted to take his mobile phone, an error that he was later to regret. He walked briskly down the road without a backward glance and half hoped that Bartholomew was not with him. He was disappointed; he caught sight of the now all too familiar figure of the Gaijin ghost by his side.

The morning was cold but bright, and the winter sun did its best to make an appearance from behind a bank of low clouds that drifted across the grey blue sky. Kiyoshi decided that he would converse with Bartholomew as little as possible as he assumed that if he was the only one able to see the manifestation, then he would look ridiculous if he mouthed off into space. Although with the invention of mobile phones it was not unusual to see a person immersed in conversation that gave the impression that he spoke to himself.

The aroma of barbecued chicken assailed his nostrils; such delicacies as Yakitori (Chicken kebab and liver with a sweet sauce skewered on sticks served with onions), but he resisted the temptation, gave a quick nod to the purveyor and strode hurriedly past to avoid any conversation.

The proprietor of the stall was too busy in preparation for the day's diners to notice Kiyoshi's reluctance to stop and converse as he had done in the past. Kiyoshi looked over his shoulder for a change in the stallholder's expression but it gave no indication that he could see anything unusual, a person with the appearance of a homeless man for example, in the company of Kiyoshi.

'Nice day,' Bartholomew commented. Kiyoshi resisted the temptation to reply, nodded and hummed a tune he'd heard earlier on the radio the night before. He was struck by a sudden thought. His mobile phone.

'Damn I left the bloody thing at home!' he exclaimed in a loud voice, and did the very thing he wished to avoid.

'Sir, is there something that ails you?' Bartholomew enquired unable to understand his language but aware of Kiyoshi's attitude.

Kiyoshi did not want a lengthy conversation and replied, 'Oh ano it is nothing, I er nearly fell.'

They made their way toward a small bridge, crossed a stream that ran under the road, turned left and followed a path parallel to

Inconvenience

the slow flowing water. Several large Koi carp swam against the current to browse in a group close to the river bank.

In spring this pedestrian passage would be ablaze with the blossom of cherry trees that lined the route, now only stark leafless branches stood like broken down sentinels on either side, and conveyed none of the beauty that lay dormant within.

Kiyoshi could see Bartholomew in his peripheral vision and looked down at his feet curious to see if they made contact with the earth. They appeared to do so but didn't leave any prints. There was also no sound of his companion's movement as his ethereal form travelled in unison with his own.

They walked, or perhaps covered would be more appropriate in Bartholomew's case, a mile or so and followed the stream as it meandered through the village. Numerous cyclists and elderly ladies, some bent almost double with age, went about their daily business. Kiyoshi regarded each individual with an obvious stare to gauge their reaction. In most cases there was none, and in those that did show some sign of a change of expression it was in response to Kiyoshi's intense gaze into their face.

Bartholomew had remained silent for most of the journey only to add the odd comment about how the Dutch should never be trusted, and the length of time he'd spent in a state of spiritual limbo because of them. Kiyoshi had never met a Dutch person and the only thing he knew about them was that they lived a long way from where he did, wore clogs and made a lot of cheese; and some child stuck his finger in a leaky flood prevention construction. As far as he was concerned their geographical location was comfortably far enough away to prohibit a sudden influx of Dutch people, a bunch of foreigners with strange habits, like all Gaijin, peculiar.

The cold had caused Kiyoshi's proboscis to exude a droplet of moisture that as he walked swung precariously from the tip.

'You've got mucus on the end of your beak man,' Bartholomew boomed.

Kiyoshi and the Grumpy Ghost

'Huh?' Kiyoshi replied and realised he had again done the very thing he set out not to do.

'Mucus, a drop of water from the contents of your nose hangs from the tip, do something about it man it irritates me, it reminds me of the first mate on a ship I once served who constantly exuded copious amounts of liquid from his oversized one.'

Kiyoshi again found it difficult to decipher exactly what Bartholomew had said but heard the word nose and was acutely aware that his own nasal organ was under close scrutiny from his ethereal companion. He raised his hand and with the part of it that the human race is said to be more familiar with than any known thing, drew it across his nostrils and took the drop of moisture with it.

'Have you not a kerchief on your person sir?' Bartholomew enquired, his expression beneath his beard one of disapproval.

'Huh?' Kiyoshi responded.

'Nevermind it is of little consequence.'

Kiyoshi turned in the direction of his unwanted companion but resisted the temptation to speak.

They continued to walk for another half mile when Kiyoshi stopped. He stood not far from a fenced off area that enclosed an oval in which several children played despite the inclement weather. There was also a track for people to run around the perimeter, the brown soil, once grass, eroded by the numerous feet that had hopped, skipped, shuffled and pounded it in the course of the earlier season.

In post dawn morning, the park was a hive of activity, elderly people stretched and exercised to the strains of Japanese style music along the lines of Enka, a kind of soul music for the over fifties, that lyrically tells of unrequited love or other misfortunes on the path of life. Others walked their dogs armed with the compulsory "Poopa scoopa" that ensured that in most cases the beloved pet's turd never hit the ground but dropped harmlessly on to the outstretched shovel that hovered beneath its sphincter as it

Inconvenience

ejected the waste matter. The dog probably disconcerted to discover that there is no sign of the recently despatched log, as canines seem to take enthusiastic interest in anything that occurs at the rear end of their own, or in fact anything else's backside. For humans it insured that in the course of their jogs, baseball practice, football practice or whatever, the ground was considerably more wholesome to make contact with.

On this occasion the only occupants of the park were Kiyoshi, Bartholomew and a group of children on the oval.

'I can feel something,' Bartholomew exclaimed.

Kiyoshi cast a hasty glance in all directions satisfying himself that the children were too far away to discern any odd behaviour on his part.

He shouldn't have worried they were too engrossed in their own activities to notice his.

'What can feel?' he replied. 'You recognise anything?'

Bartholomew gazed straight ahead.

'The place is unfamiliar to me. I can see nothing that I recognise but I can feel that I am very close.'

Bartholomew turned toward the conveniences that lay to their left and walked toward them. Kiyoshi watched and then followed. Bartholomew drifted into the small brick enclosure and disappeared from view into the ladies' section. Kiyoshi followed; as he neared the entrance he heard a loud roar.

'They are here! I've found them.'

Kiyoshi raced into the toilet and half expected to see a skeleton in the middle of the floor. Instead he was confronted by the sight of Bartholomew staring at the ground in a state of excitement. Kiyoshi followed his companion's gaze but failed to see anything other than the concrete floor.

'They are interned in this very spot I know it.'

'You mean bones are in this place?'

Kiyoshi and the Grumpy Ghost

'Yes sir in this very place beneath my feet.'

Kiyoshi's mind began to respond to the information that had just been presented and the results of his mental processes did not encourage him.

'But if bones are here how can I dig up?' he enquired.

'Ground very hard cannot just dig'.

'Why not?'

'Because very, very strong ground, this not just earth, this very strong earth.'

Kiyoshi had no idea whether Bartholomew had any knowledge of concrete and was not sure how long it had been used to build houses especially in the West. He knew that the Romans had it, and houses built in England in the Elizabethan period were constructed of more than mud or clay or for that matter many castles, but what the actual materials they were built with and their similarity to the technology of today he had no knowledge.

Bartholomew regarded the balding Japanese man.

'I am aware sir of the difficulty that you must overcome, but I ask you please try and solve this problem.

'But how? I no can dig this, I have no tool to do this.' An idea struck Kiyoshi.

'Only one person can help. A Mr Takashi he very influencing person.'

'I think the word you are looking for is influential, and why can this man help?'

'He is councillor person he can do things, can dig toilets.'

'Why cannot you ask him?' Bartholomew replied. 'And what are toilets?'

'He won't believe if I tell,' Kiyoshi replied, and went on to give an explanation as best he could with regard to the function of toilets.

Inconvenience

Bartholomew thought for a moment.

'Very well then I will speak with this man, where can I find him?'

Kiyoshi felt as though a weight had been lifted off his back, a sense of relief swept over him as he heard the words.

He didn't like Mr Takashi although he had been a friend of his father. He was a surly rude man who always looked for an opportunity to make money or climb into the panties of any woman that gave him the chance. He, also much to Kiyoshi's horror, although considerably older, had taken a shine to Kaoru, another reason for his dislike of the man.

'Where can I find him?' Bartholomew repeated.

Kiyoshi looked at his unwanted companion and wondered what the disadvantages the state of ghostliness held.

It offered free and rapid travel, no living costs, no tiresome bodily functions, and no deterioration of the mental state. The ability to appear and vanish apparently at will, the lack of necessity to work, and immortality to boot. Why did the spectre seem so miserable with his condition?

'Mr Takashi lives very close my house. I take you there.'

Kiyoshi was about to explain in greater detail as to the exact location of his neighbour when he noticed the familiar shape of a small girl standing in the entrance of the convenience. She was wrapped in warm clothes and her breath clearly visible as she watched in silence the strange behaviour of one of her teachers.

'Well what do you want?' Kiyoshi asked in an unfriendly manner.

'Please sir I want to go the toilet.'

Kiyoshi realised where he was.

'Oh, er, yes of course carry on I was just checking something I thought I heard a noise.'

'Yes sir,' she replied and made her way over to the nearest cubicle.

Kiyoshi cleared his throat in the manner of a professor about to address a group of students, and moved toward the exit. Bartholomew had remained silent during the small girl's interruption but now continued to vocalise his thoughts.

'It would be most appreciated if you would direct me to this Mr Tashaki.'

'Takashi,' Kiyoshi corrected.

'Takashi,' Bartholomew repeated.

'Are you sure he is the right person to lend assistance?'

'Most surely *yes.*' Kiyoshi emphasised the word yes.

'In that case let us delay no further, let us to this Mr Takashi with all haste.'

Kiyoshi again did not understand Bartholomew's every word but gathered by what had been discussed, and the urgency in his voice, that he was anxious to meet Mr Takashi. Kiyoshi was also motivated to rid himself of his companion.

He strode from the convenience and was met on the way out by a group of girls on their way in from the oval.

Kiyoshi stared straight ahead and increased his pace. A voice spoke from within the gaggle of young girls.

'Good morning Mr. Hirota.' There was almost an air of impudence in the tone. Kiyoshi said nothing but felt the hairs at the base of his neck tingle as the situation of his location and circumstances presented itself to his consciousness. When school resumed he would have to face the consequences of this moment and student smirks throughout the playground.

He had travelled a few yards from the building when he heard squeals of girlish laughter ring out across the park and imagined, correctly as it happened, the first visitor to the wash basins had informed her companions of his earlier "strange" behaviour.

Inconvenience

Despite the extreme chill of the winter's day his face became hot and glowed from embarrassment at the prospect of forthcoming ridicule.

'Delightful children,' Bartholomew said.

Kiyoshi continued without a comment but in his mind he was, most of the time of a different opinion.

They walked back along the banks of the stream beneath the stark shapes of the naked trees, Kiyoshi's head bowed against the wind. The tinkle of a bicycle bell would occasionally request him to step aside for the passage of a rugged up rider battling the elements in a quest for some item of shopping or on a visit to a neighbour.

"Soy sauce," Kiyoshi thought, changed direction and headed toward the supermarket. It wasn't far and offered some shelter from the cold and would please his mother. A reason for her to think well of his behaviour was not something that occurred very often.

Flakes of snow began to fall, whipped and tossed in their descent by gusts adding to the discomfort of the day. Kiyoshi reached the area where the majority of the village shops were located. A small post office, a bank, a bakery, and a fishmonger that displayed several varieties of fish laid out in neat rows, eyes staring into space, particles of ice still frozen on the shiny bodies a testimony to the bite of the north wind.

Outside the supermarket were bicycles some neatly parked others draped over the railings that separated the footpath from the road. The smell of freshly cooked Oban-yaki, a sweet bun, assailed the nostrils of the passers-by as they entered and left the store; their taste buds stimulated by the purveyor to induce them to part with their hard earned yen.

Kiyoshi felt hungry; the prospect of Bartholomew's departure combined with the sharp chill of the day had stimulated his appetite, plus he'd hardly eaten much breakfast that morning. Bartholomew was agitated.

'Is this Mr Tashaki?' he asked.

'Takashi,' Kiyoshi replied and remembered to any onlooker he, to all appearance, addressed empty space.

'Pardon?' replied the stallholder.

'Takashi then. Is this him?' continued Bartholomew.

'No not him, ar…no ahemm.' Kiyoshi emulated his first statement but distorted it to sound as though he wanted to clear his throat. The Oban-yaki seller looked at Kiyoshi not convinced he hadn't spoken.

'Yes sir, what would you like?' the stallholder enquired.

'Oban-yaki please, just one.'

'What are we doing here may I ask, I thought we were on our way to the house of Mr Takashi?' Bartholomew stated, a note of frustration in his voice.

Kiyoshi ignored him and focused his attention on the preparation of his bun.

'Sir if you continue to ignore me I shall give your ear a very painful tweak.'

Kiyoshi felt almost smug and was about to receive the hot aromatic sweetmeat when he felt his left ear, already half frozen with cold, drop a degree lower in temperature and twist violently to the left. The stallholder's gaze alighted on the revolving ear as he passed the Oban-yaki to him.

Noting the man's expression, he knew that his ear was the subject of scrutiny. His eyes widened and with tremendous control he managed to stifle a scream of agony, grit his teeth and display a warm smile. The stall holder confronted by a man who, leaned toward him with eyes that almost popped out of his head, a face contorted by an inane grin whilst their left ear practised aerobics, caused him to believe that he was in the presence of a lunatic or someone of a slightly unbalanced nature. Kiyoshi took the hot bun, handed over the exact amount required to purchase the delicacy, and managed to relay a message of thanks through his clenched teeth. The stallholder grinned back and subconsciously, tried to emulate his customer. He lifted the right side of his mouth

Inconvenience

and closed his eye in an effort to stimulate his own ear into some kind of motion. Kiyoshi ignored him and turned away. Bartholomew released his grip, Kiyoshi rubbed his ear, which if nothing else had become decidedly warmer.

'Why you do that?' Kiyoshi shouted totally forgetful of his resolve to refrain from communication in public.

'Because my dear sir, when I speak to you I expect the courtesy of an answer.'

'But I just buy mother soya sauce.' Kiyoshi responded.

The Oban-yaki vendor a few feet away stared in Kiyoshi's direction with curiosity as he endeavoured to emulate the contorted ear trick. Kiyoshi's loud and apparent conversation with himself had stimulated his interest even more.

'The last words you spoke to me sir, were that you were going to show me the whereabouts of one Mr Takashi and then the next thing when I politely enquire of our whereabouts in relation to the aforementioned you choose to totally ignore me and purchase victuals. Thus my irritation and the tweak of your ear to which I might add I gave you due warning.'

'I was go to Mr Takashi place but mother asked me to buy soy sauce, so first I buy and then go Mr Takashi,' Kiyoshi blurted and rubbed his offended ear with one hand and held the hot bun in the other.

'Well why didn't you inform me of this in the first place then I would know of your intentions and show a little patience.'

Kiyoshi looked about him, a few people went in and out of the supermarket but only the stallholder had noticed his conversation with Bartholomew and chatted to a prospective buyer with gestures to his ear and a nod in the direction of Kiyoshi.

'And besides sir, if I might add the object that you have purchased has more consistency than a sauce. It looks to me to be a cake of some kind.'

'This Oban-yaki,' Kiyoshi replied. He was about to offer to purchase another for Bartholomew when he thought better of it and decided it may be indiscreet. He was puzzled that Bartholomew could physically touch him and wondered how it was possible, if he was, as he said, not of this plane.

'Oan aki,' Bartholomew repeated.

'Oban-yaki,' Kiyoshi corrected. 'Like, er, cake, I was hungry and today cold, so I need to eating. I go into shop and buy sauce.'

He turned, walked into the supermarket passed the curious stallholder about to pay the price of his attention to Kiyoshi's behaviour by neglect of his own business. In his efforts to ascertain whether Kiyoshi was insane he had failed to notice that his latest batch of Oban-yaki were already past the point of "cooked" and now entered the stage when to swear and curse would have little effect, nor change their colour from the charcoal grey they now assumed. Nevertheless, the stallholder gave a valiant attempt, and mouthed off words that cannot easily be found in the Japanese dictionary as he prized the blackened buns from the tray.

Kiyoshi nodded politely as he entered. Bartholomew followed him in. The automatic doors closed behind them and Kiyoshi felt the change of temperature as he moved away from the entrance. He made a beeline for the aisle with the sauces and soups. His purposeful gait was brought to a sudden halt as he caught sight of Kaoru next to the tofu counter.

He turned and fondled a packet of rice flakes on the middle shelves and pretended to be deeply engrossed in the artwork on the packet. Bartholomew was otherwise engaged and removed a plastic container of mayonnaise close to the spot where Kiyoshi feigned interest in the flakes.

Kiyoshi could see Bartholomew from his peripheral vision and took little notice until he was aware that an elderly man gaped in disbelief at a bottle that apparently hovered unsuspended a foot or so away from the nearest shelf.

Inconvenience

His mind was preoccupied by what to say to her when the realisation that the old boy might draw attention to the phenomena brought him back to reality and motivated him to take action.

Kiyoshi walked to the location of the levitated sauce, stretched out his hand, placed his finger and thumb around the stem of the container and held it out at arm's length, so as not to snatch it from Bartholomew's grasp. The fear of another tweak prompted his caution. Bartholomew regarded his companion.

'Precisely what are you doing sir?' he enquired. Kiyoshi smiled at the old gentleman and nodded his head as he tried to think how he could answer whilst he was still under scrutiny. An idea struck him; he peered intently at the mayonnaise and then spoke very slowly as if he read the label.

'Please no touch Barslomo san, make people look, no good for me.'

Bartholomew shrugged but understood Kiyoshi's point.

'Very well as you wish but can we please make haste and meet this Mr Takayashi?'

Kiyoshi didn't bother to correct his mispronunciation but nodded in the direction of his ethereal colleague, a slow nod, for the sake of the onlooker as much as anything else. He hoped to give the impression that he was satisfied as to the contents of the bottle, and in agreement with what was contained within as a prerequisite for purchase.

The old man shuffled past him without a word and turned into the next aisle. Kiyoshi replaced the mayonnaise and looked toward the tofu counter.

Kaoru had moved on. He felt anxious; his heart rate increased with every step towards the spot where the vision of loveliness had vacated. He hardly dared turn the corner; he stopped and took a deep breath. Bartholomew drifted on ahead. Kiyoshi negotiated the corner and nearly collided with the old man as he shuffled back down the aisle toward him. He managed to avoid contact and apologised as he continued his quest for the sight of the heavenly entity that glided with the grace of a gazelle between the displays

Kiyoshi and the Grumpy Ghost

of fruit, vegetables, washing powder and all the other items that adorned the racks and shelves of the store.

'What exactly are we looking for?' Bartholomew asked with a hint of impatience in his voice. Kiyoshi looked quickly in each direction.

'I get soy sauce, it er ano around next aisle.'

'Then please sir, get it and let us be on our way.'

Kiyoshi understood perfectly well his companions request and thought perhaps the best course of action would be to forgo the chance to speak to Kaoru and get rid of his uninvited guest as soon as possible, after all it was the top of his priority list, and would allow his life to return to a semblance of normality. He tried to recollect the exact location of the soy sauce; he had formed a mental picture as to its whereabouts, when a soft voice fell on his ear and caused his whole body to tingle as if a mild electrical current had passed through him. He began to wax poetical. The sound of bells, the summer's gentle breeze through the willow leaves, the ripple of waves on the shoreline, or the trickle of water from a mountain stream, could never sound half as sweet as the voice that vibrated his eardrum.

He turned and was greeted by the face of Kaoru. The sight of those dark eyes and the flash of her beautiful white teeth encased by full red lips, made his heart miss a beat and that part of his anatomy involved in the reproductive process when stimulated into the correct proportion, twitched as if in anticipation of the fulfilment of his wildest fantasy. A hot flush swept through him.

'Oh er hi,' he blurted out. 'Er how are you?'

'I am very well thank you, and how is your mother?'

Kaoru answered and sent varied sensations through Kiyoshi as well as the odd twitch of the previously mentioned organ which had begun to involuntarily expand.

'Oh she is fine, yes very well, thank you.' Kiyoshi turned his gaze away from Kaoru aware that he stared too hard.

Inconvenience

'Are you not working today?' he asked desperate to prolong the moment spent in the presence of such beauty.

'Yes, I am just buying a few things for the office. When do you return to school?'

'Next week,' Kiyoshi replied.

'Are you pleased to be going back?' Kaoru asked, her hand moved to her brow, slender fingers stroked a hair away from her face.

Kiyoshi noticed the movement and the delicacy of its execution. He had been aware of the wayward strand and thought it would be a desirable situation to be in the position of familiarity to reach out and brush the irritation away. If he conducted such a move now, he would probably cause her alarm at such forwardness and ruin any chance to fulfil his fantasies of romance.

He was about to answer Kaoru when he was reminded of the necessity to rid himself of an ethereal entity. Bartholomew had remained patient whilst Kiyoshi went through the pleasantries of polite conversation but now was less tolerant as time progressed.

'My dear sir, I do not wish to be rude but I would like to remind you that there is a certain matter in hand that needs our attention.'

Kiyoshi gathered by Bartholomew's tone that he wanted to move on. Again he was confronted by the decision to ignore him and risk the painful reprimand with a tweaked ear.

Alternatively, to give an answer, could convey the wrong impression to the object of his desire and infer that he suffered some form of mental illness or schizophrenia; a risk not to be taken at this stage of the relationship. He felt a tingle run up and down his vertebra, but it was one of apprehension rather than fright; his imagination presented him with a mental image of some part of his anatomy being manipulated by ghostly fingers.

'Please excuse me I really must go I have an urgent appointment,' Kiyoshi blurted out, the words in contradiction to his thoughts.

Kiyoshi and the Grumpy Ghost

Kaoru gave a shallow bow and stepped aside to let him pass.

'It was nice to see you again,' she said.

Kiyoshi returned the bow and inclined the upper half of his body toward her.

'It was my pleasure,' he replied with all sincerity. He hurried from her to the soy sauce shelf, grasped the nearest bottle, made for the checkout counter and turned only to give a quick nod to Bartholomew that he was leaving.

He found it hard to believe that the great big hairy ghost of Bartholomew was invisible to everybody else but himself.

As the girl swiped the label of the soy sauce over the scanner Kiyoshi looked into her face. The only thing she registered was an expression that indicated to him, her perception of most things was none too acute, let alone the existence of anything paranormal.

Bartholomew viewed the scene in the supermarket with indifference, but demonstrated interest in the cash registers and automatic doors. Kiyoshi on the other hand had kept an eye on his vaporous colleague and noted his curiosity. He also maintained a furtive vigil for the lovely Kaoru but exited before she had completed her errand.

It was snowing; many of the prospective shoppers had snowflake dotted umbrellas. As they entered they shook them out, either placed them in a rack provided or covered them, to avoid drips of water in the shop, with a tube of plastic large enough to be used as an equine condom.

Kiyoshi passed the rack, stretched out his arm, lifted the nearest umbrella, opened it and walked away. It was not an expensive article but it was not his, therefore a theft of someone else's property. Bartholomew said nothing.

Kiyoshi forged his way through a flurry of snow. The north wind increased; he strove to keep the plastic of the umbrella intact to provide him some meagre protection from the elements.

Inconvenience

In contrast Bartholomew glided alongside him, unaffected by the turmoil of the gale, his clothes and hair unruffled.

Kiyoshi's mind worked overtime, thoughts of Kaoru and the opportunity to ask her out had been lost by the impatience of a spirit. "How would he rid himself of this ethereal curse and introduce him to Mr Takashi? Perhaps the best plan would be to identify him from afar, point him out to Bartholomew who could then introduce himself." His reverie was interrupted by the sound of his companion's voice above the howl of the wind.

'You like that wench, I gather.'

Kiyoshi turned.

'Eh?' he responded and raised his own voice in competition with the gale.

'The woman, you like her?' Bartholomew repeated.

'No I just know her from living around same place,' Kiyoshi denied.

'I don't believe you, I can tell when a man desires a woman and you behaved like a love sick bull.'

Kiyoshi said nothing, his attention directed to a more immediate matter, to stop his umbrella turning inside out by a strong gust of wind.

CHAPTER 3

The confession

"How I hate winter," thought Kiyoshi as the snow increased in density and swirls of flakes settled to form a carpet of white over the path, that by evening would turn to ice and make it difficult for the elderly to negotiate.

Kiyoshi headed toward the Sakura bank and went through the automatic doors.

On the opposite side of the road a red faced man, another purveyor of Oban yaki, hoped that the elements would stimulate sales as they'd not sold exactly as hot cakes are supposed to.

It was not the bank proper but an area designated for dispensation or to deposit cash via several machines lined against the walls. Kiyoshi took out his card, approached one of the automatic tellers and turned toward Bartholomew as he did so.

'I come here to talk with you. Takashi san office opposite; next to Oban-yaki seller. I describe and you go meet.'

'No I think it better if you come with me and then explain to this Mr Tashaki.'

Kiyoshi was none too keen on the idea of:

a} an encounter with Takashi;

b} to have to explain that a ghost paid him a visit and asked for help, whom he redirected to his doorstep and gave him a problem he no doubt didn't want.

'No maybe better you on own I think,' Kiyoshi reiterated.

'No maybe better you come too,' Bartholomew said emulating Kiyoshi.

The confession

Kiyoshi regarded the ethereal figure as he casually leaned on one of the machines and decided that if he were to be rid of this ghostly menace it would be the best policy to go along with the spook's wishes. Kiyoshi drew his coat around himself and fumbled with the handle of his recently acquired umbrella. He gave a simple nod and strode from the bank.

The icy blast of the north wind lashed him anew as a flurry of snowflakes danced around the side of his erect gamp. He bent forward, braved the elements and made it across the road into the building of the unpleasant Mr Takashi.

The receptionist looked up as Kiyoshi entered and the warmth of the air conditioning temporarily subsided as the doors opened and closed to allow the chill of winter a brief moment of indulgence. If the receptionist experienced any discomfort from the icy blast that must have caressed her ankles, she didn't show it but politely bowed and bade Kiyoshi welcome.

'I would like to see Mr Takashi if I may?' Kiyoshi stated.

'I'm sorry sir, Mr. Takashi is in a meeting at the moment and I have instructions not to disturb him.'

'How long will he be?' Kiyoshi asked.

'I have no idea, but he has several engagements today and he is already running late, please excuse me,' she replied and reached for the telephone as it emitted a high pitched ring. Kiyoshi turned to Bartholomew who peered at the receptionist. He wondered how he could relate the information without the appearance that he talked to himself. He bowed politely to the girl and without a word made a hasty exit through the doors, braved the elements and ran across the road to gain shelter in the bank previously occupied.

Kiyoshi could see whilst he spoke to the receptionist that the bank building was unoccupied and it would offer him the opportunity to impart the information he had gleaned to Bartholomew, whom he thought would no doubt, because of his actions execute another ear tweak.

Kiyoshi and the Grumpy Ghost

Bartholomew was indeed perplexed and confronted Kiyoshi as he entered the building.

'Why sir did you make such a hasty exit from Tashaki's place?' Bartholomew enquired.

Kiyoshi closed the umbrella and shook it.

'Takashi san is in meeting and very busy person.'

Bartholomew looked at Kiyoshi.

'Busy you say, well we will see about that.'

'I no can meet Takashi san for maybe one day. If you like I make date for seeing er appointment,' Kiyoshi responded, grateful if only for the moment, that he had been spared the ordeal of an introduction of an ethereal being to a person he considered to be his rival for the affections of the woman he loved.

'Maybe you visit is better, he has room on number five floor er number of room is 512,' Kiyoshi uttered.

He sensed that Bartholomew was resolved to see Takashi and in the process hoped it would release him from his company in the process. Bartholomew stroked his hirsute chin and vanished. Kiyoshi looked across the road at the Takashi building to see if his companion would materialise there. He didn't. As he stared across the windswept road, a car or truck would hiss by to obscure his line of vision.

Outside, the snow whirled around and resembled a small round glass ball he once had when he was a child; inside there was a man and a woman holding hands. When the ball was turned upside down or shaken the appearance of a downfall of snow would swirl around the motionless couple. Kiyoshi was always fascinated by the silence of the tiny artificial flakes as they fell to settle on the bottom of the glass; he would hold it to his ear whilst the contrived fall drifted downward and yielded, despite its minuscule weight, to the pull of gravity. He likened himself to one of the figures in the globe and wished he had the figure of Kaoru beside him.

The confession

Whilst Kiyoshi daydreamed, Bartholomew had at that moment materialised in front of Mr Takashi. In itself it would have been shock enough to the overweight business man but Mr Takashi was in a position of compromise when the appearance of the hairy Gaijin in his office proved too much for his already overworked heart. The meeting that the business man attended was that of his genitalia with those of his secretary whilst she bent over the desk, her clothes suitably arranged in order to accommodate the amorous thrust of Mr Takashi's loins.

Because of their position they both faced the same way, the man's face twisted in a lustful grimace as his energetic grind came to a climax on the "vinegar strokes", as they are sometimes referred to by sailors and others of a less gentile nature to describe the act of sexual intercourse as it draws to its conclusion.

The secretary's visage was obscured as she looked downward as the ample stomach of Takashi slapped with rhythmic regularity against her exposed buttocks and caused her to brace herself in order to prevent being shoved across to the opposite side of the table.

Bartholomew appeared directly in front of the couple; he took a step forward, his bearded face topped with a mass of unkempt hair added to the shock of his materialisation.

'Tashaki, er Takashi?' he boomed inches from the grimace of the face that had now suddenly lost its lustful expression and instead had assumed one of total shock. Takashi managed to elicit a startled gasp before he succumbed to the realisation that there was a third person or something that resembled one in his presence at a time when it was least desirable and that he, or whatever it was, addressed him by his own name. The stress of the situation was too much and the heart of Mr. Takashi revolted at the amount of effort required to pump blood rapidly through the already congested arteries; it stopped beating.

He slumped forward on to his unfortunate partner, his arms locked around her waist in a grip of death. The secretary assumed that her boss had ejaculated and rested from the effort. The first inclination she had that all was not as it should be, was when, after a few moments she requested he resume a more comfortable position. No response. He clung to her as an amorous toad fixed to a reluctant recipient of its lust, often a fish, his expression equally as glassy-eyed. She turned her head in order to see his face but could only see the top of his head his features buried in her back. She tried to release the grip of his arms around her waist but his last muscle spasm had locked him solid and it would take the strength of at least two men to release her. She began to panic; she realised her position, aware she could no longer feel the movement of his intake of breath. The conclusion that she was in the embrace of a corpse motivated her to drag herself and her now deceased lover across to the telephone: she pressed the necessary numbers; it would secure her release although at the same time bring her endless embarrassment and without doubt the butt of jokes and office gossip for years to come, as well as the loss of the pay increase the now deceased Mr Takashi had promised.

Bartholomew had watched the departure of Takashi's spirit and acknowledged him, his destination many fleshy recycles before the dawn of his enlightenment.

The late Takashi seemed none too pleased as he embarked on his spiritual adventure but as the burden of the physical plane with its thousand shocks and heartaches dropped away, a radiant light engulfed him and he assumed an altogether brighter aspect as he continued his journey.

Kiyoshi gazed out of the bank window and thought he had been released from the responsibility of his unwanted companion when Bartholomew appeared next to him. He was startled; although now comparatively used to the fact that he had communication with an entity from the "other side", the sudden appearance of the bearded ghost still caused his brain to register the phenomena in a negative way.

'I wish you no appear like that. It very make me shocked,' he continued. 'What happen with Takashi san?'

'Ah, a most unfortunate or perhaps fortunate, depending how you look at it, situation.'

The confession

'I no understand,' Kiyoshi said, not sure of Bartholomew's words.

'You see Takashi san, he see you?'

'Yes but that was the problem, I think my appearance could have been premature under the circumstances.'

Bartholomew assumed an expression of innocence hidden under the mass of hair, undetected by the school teacher.

Kiyoshi's ability to fulfil Bartholomew's demands seemed to diminish by the minute.

'Takashi no help you? What did he say?'

'Unfortunately he didn't say a great deal before he died.'

'Died!' Kiyoshi repeated. 'You mean Takashi san dead?'

'Yes I'm afraid that is the case,' Bartholomew said wistfully.

'Why he die?' Kiyoshi asked, aware that Bartholomew could utilise objects and use force on the physical plane as manifested earlier by his revolving ear.

'The shock of seeing me,' Bartholomew replied omitting to tell Kiyoshi the complete story.

Kiyoshi nodded as he listened, he could understand that the sight of Bartholomew's sudden appearance was enough to give anyone a heart attack.

'So once more dear sir I am in your hands to aid me to find peace and freedom from this earthly bondage.'

Although Kiyoshi caught a scant amount of what Bartholomew said, he understood enough to realise that he was saddled with the hairy ghost.

Gloom and despondency crept over him, seasoned with a twinge of guilt that he wasn't saddened by the sudden departure of Mr. Takashi: a few moments ago his formidable rival for Kaoru's affection, the salvation of his predicament, the person who could have released him from the curse of Bartholomew's presence. Dead.

Kiyoshi and the Grumpy Ghost

His mind grappled for a solution to the problem of exhumation of Bartholomew's bones. He cast a glance at his intangible colleague and could see by his posture he was not happy.

Outside, the weather improved, the wind had dropped and allowed the snow to fall gently to earth from the grey sky to give the impression the street was covered in talcum powder. Kiyoshi exited the bank and raised his umbrella, his mind on the problem of Bartholomew. His reverie consumed his attention and took his mind from the needs of the moment. Without a thought he stepped into the path of a truck. The driver slammed on the brakes, skidded out of control and spun in his direction. As the side of the vehicle was about to collide with his person and facilitate a face to face encounter with Mr Takashi, he was lifted over the truck and into the air engulfed, in a strange blue light; he landed with the grace of an Olympic gymnast on the other side of the road. The truck managed to avoid a collision and shuddered to a halt; the shaken driver emerged from the cabin.

To the only witness of the event Kiyoshi had by some superhuman effort leapt over the truck on one side of the road and landed on the other.

The Oban-yaki seller, a few yards from Takashi's office block, rubbed his eyes in disbelief and dropped his jaw to reveal several gold fillings. Kiyoshi stood on unsteady legs and re-orientated himself; he remained still as he tried to work out how he got there. The driver was upset and made no secret of it to Kiyoshi who bowed apologetically as the irate face gradually resumed its normal expression; the contracted muscles relaxed as the anger and indignation of the shock that he'd nearly killed someone subsided.

Kiyoshi waited until the tirade of abuse abated and the driver climbed back into his truck before his mind began to reorganise his thoughts and convey to him his next move.

He realised that Bartholomew had saved his life, but by the same token he would not have crossed the road on such a cold and miserable day, if he hadn't been there because of him. He sought to ascertain the presence of his saviour and located the hirsute

The confession

face a foot or so from his own. He recoiled at the sudden shock of the ghostly visage at such close proximity.

'What happen?' he asked.

'I saved you from that thing that bore down upon you,' Bartholomew replied with a smug look on his face only visible by the twinkle in his eyes. Kiyoshi worked out his colleague's words and bowed rather grudgingly.

'Thank you,' he muttered but refrained to add that it was Bartholomew's fault that he was in such a situation to begin with; he decided it would lead to further discussion and was aware that the Oban-yaki seller now watched him with more than just casual interest.

'Well sir, what now?' Bartholomew asked.

The weather had taken a turn for the worse and a flurry of windswept snow caused Kiyoshi to screw up his eyes in an effort to avoid the lash of the elements.

'What mean?' he responded.

'What do we do now?' Bartholomew emphasised and spoke each word in order for Kiyoshi to understand.

'What can do, how can help? Maybe I can do nothing.'

Bartholomew eyed his companion.

'There's gratitude for you. I save your life and you are reluctant to help me.' He shook his head and sighed. Kiyoshi felt guilty.

'O.K. I try think please give me time a little. Come, my house tonight when mother in bed we can talk, please.'

Kiyoshi looked into Bartholomew's face, which despite being between him and the cold wind, offered no resistance to the icy air that buffered him. Bartholomew could see that Kiyoshi needed time to come up with a solution; he nodded in agreement.

'As you wish good sir, until tonight then.'

Kiyoshi and the Grumpy Ghost

Kiyoshi bowed automatically, quickly put his hand on the back of his neck and rubbed it as if to indicate that the inclination of his head was to relieve some discomfort in that region of his body.

Bartholomew faded from sight; The Oban-yaki seller peered intently at Kiyoshi, perhaps in anticipation of a leap over some other vehicle. Kiyoshi was quickly gaining a reputation for unusual activity among the various stall holders. He pulled his coat firmly around himself, and headed home to the warmth of the heated table, where he would place his legs and sit like some pampered sultan to watch the lunch time news on N.H.K.

Kiyoshi's mother continued to attend to her domestic chores when he arrived, and although the pleasure of the table beckoned him on his homeward journey, his thoughts were on the problem of how to rid himself of Bartholomew, how the community would react to the death of Mr Takashi; he decided to remain silent about the affair plus any knowledge of it.

Kiyoshi sat down to lunch and toyed listlessly with his noodles, the chopsticks held loosely between his fingers, he turned to his mother.

'If someone saved a member of our family's life would we be obligated to help them?'

His mother slurped her noodles noisily and regarded her son with suspicion.

'What do you mean?'

'If someone for example helped one of our ancestors or even me, saved their life, then would we be obligated to help them?' Kiyoshi stated.

His mother looked blankly at her son.

'Are you being serious? If someone saves your life then I would have thought that you would want to help them, whether it's an obligation or not is a matter for your own conscience.'

She was about to enquire further as to the reason why he asked, in her opinion, such a stupid question, when she realised

The confession

from past experience any effort to extract information from him was futile, and returned to her meal.

Kiyoshi stared blankly into space and mulled over his obligation to Bartholomew. It made the task seem even more odious. "What could he do? He was not physically able to dig through concrete without the aid of some mechanical device."

He visualised himself behind the controls of a pneumatic drill and shuddered at the thought albeit less violently than if he had wrestled with one. The whole thing was preposterous; he could no more operate a drill of such power as fly to the moon.

His mother continued to shovel in her noodles, her chopsticks moved similar to a pair of knitting needles from bowl to face. She occasionally regarded her son in the process but refrained to make any comment even when he grimaced as his mind conjured up images of himself vibrating behind a dirty great machine that thumped up and down in order to drill a hole in the ladies' toilet.

"How could he possibly gain permission to carry out such a task even if he could do it?" he thought.

As he rearranged his chopsticks between his fingers an idea came to him. If he couldn't do it himself then he would get someone else to do it for him. He had a few days left of the school holidays and the task could be completed before he was due to return.

'I'm going to Tokyo for a couple of days on business, I have to see someone about a book for school. I've telephoned a few times but it's probably best if I actually go there in person.'

His mother nodded. She didn't believe her son for a minute, firmly convinced that he was off to bonk again with someone totally unsuitable for a daughter in law.

'When are you going?' she enquired.

'First thing in the morning.' Kiyoshi replied and slurped extra loudly on the hot noodles; his mind formulated his next course of action which was to go to the local police station and put his plan into effect.

'Why two days?' his mother asked.

'I will call on a friend of mine and we'll probably go and have a meal or something.'

His mother rose from the table, picked up a small teapot and carried it to a kettle that steamed and simmered on the stove. She filled it with water and returned to the table, her expression unchanged from the stoic grimace that she generally had when she tried to prize information from her reticent offspring. Kiyoshi watched her as she poured the green liquid into his cup. It reminded him of the act of urination that in turn reminded him of the ladies' toilet where the bones of his accursed tormentor lay buried beneath several feet of concrete.

Bartholomew's presence continued to intrude upon his thoughts even by some vague association and stimulated his resolve to put his plan into effect, regardless of the consequence. To rid himself of this unwanted apparition must take precedence over everything else.

It was nine o'clock the following morning when Kiyoshi strode into the local police station. The officer behind the desk tinkered about with a bicycle and cast a quick glance over his shoulder at the sound of Kiyoshi's footsteps. He continued to fiddle around with the saddle; his intention to lower it, demonstrated by his attempt to secure a spanner around a worn nut that had been over exposed to the elements. After a few moments the police officer stood up and felt that his endeavour might be more fruitful if carried out at a later date without the inquisitive gaze of a spectator. He approached Kiyoshi.

'Yes?' he enquired.

Kiyoshi could see why he had been so engaged in an alteration to the height of the saddle. He was almost five foot in his boots. Generally Japanese police are not massive at the best of time, but this little constable looked positively elf-like in stature. Kiyoshi managed to control his surprise by the confrontation of one so small wearing the uniform of the constabulary. He regarded the man's ears to see if they were bent and distorted by years of Judo training or wrestling, they were not. His gaze then went to the

The confession

man's hands to discern if he had smashed bricks bare handed or practised push ups on his knuckles in order to harden them on the journey to master the art of Karate. They were decidedly smooth.

"He must be an Aikido practitioner," Kiyoshi surmised as there were no outward signs of any physical detriment from the practice of a Martial art.

"He had to be something." Kiyoshi was convinced that the vertically challenged policeman was indeed an expert of some kind to be in uniform.

'Yes,' he repeated, 'What can I do for you?'

'Oh, er I've come to confess a murder.'

The policeman gave no indication of surprise.

'I see and whom did you murder sir may I ask?' The problem saddle abandoned to give his full attention to Kiyoshi.

'It was a man I met in a hotel,' Kiyoshi responded.

'Perhaps you could tell me more about it sir, please come this way.'

Kiyoshi was led to a room behind the main desk; the constable explained to a senior officer of Kiyoshi's wish to make a clean breast of it. The senior officer by contrast was of formidable stature and towered over Kiyoshi; he rose from behind the table.

'A murder, hmmm please take a seat.'

Kiyoshi and the officer faced each other across the desk.

'Mifune, two coffees.'

The tiny officer bowed politely and left the office.

'Now then sir, I take it you did want coffee?'

'Oh yes, thank you,' Kiyoshi nodded.

'Now about this murder, please do go on.' The senior officer's face beamed with anticipation, he visualised himself at least in receipt of some accolade from his superiors for the detention and apprehension of a criminal, albeit one who had walked in off the street and given himself up.

'My name is Hiroki Nakayama.' He produced a business card from the right hand breast pocket of his uniform and handed it to Kiyoshi, who accepted it with due ceremony, scrutinised it with enough conviction, placed it on the table and bowed as he did so. Kiyoshi apologised for his inability to furnish him with one of his own but assured officer Nakayama that he would give him one at the first opportunity.

Kiyoshi took a deep breath.

'My name is Kiyoshi Hirota...'

The story that he told was one that concerned himself and a man he met twenty years ago in a hotel. They had been involved in conversation when Kiyoshi had become intimidated by the man's manner. When he demanded money from him, he refused and left the hotel. He was followed through the park and turned to see his tormentor brandishing a knife. A fight ensued. There was a short struggle and the outcome was that Kiyoshi accidentally stabbed his attacker and inflicted a fatal wound. It was near the entrance to the park; he dragged the body further into the darkness of the recreation ground, went home and returned with a shovel; laboured most of the night and dug as deep as time allowed before the break of dawn. He buried the corpse and threw the last shovel load of soil back into place as the first glimmer of light heralded the approach of daybreak. The officer listened attentively to Kiyoshi's story, averting his gaze from time to time, to check the tape-recorder captured his confession and to take a sip of coffee.

When Kiyoshi had finished, Nakayama leaned back. His left hand reached inside his trouser pocket and pulled out a crumpled packet of cigarettes. He fumbled with large fat fingers and managed to produce one with several wrinkles. Kiyoshi watched as the protruding pencil of tobacco was thrust in his direction.

He declined the offer.

The policeman pulled the cigarette from the packet and placed it under his nose and sniffed it.

The confession

'I really love the smell of tobacco don't you?' he enquired.

'Er yes I think it's quite pleasant,' Kiyoshi responded and wondered what exactly the man had in mind. Nakayama placed the cigarette between his lips and set fire to it; his instrument, a Zippo lighter that gave the familiar trade mark metallic sound when the flame is extinguished, by a flick of the wrist, a movement that adds drama to any moment. Kiyoshi wondered how many impressionable youths had taken up cigarettes in order to emulate their cinematic hero, with a quick snap shut of their Zippo before they embarked upon some venture, or sucked the face of some luscious co- star.

The police officer's cheeks hollowed as he drew the smoke into his lungs, Kiyoshi half expected to see it come out of his ears. Eventually the exhalation came with sound similar to an espresso coffee machine, smoke billowed out with enough "drama" to have made Humphrey Bogart envious.

'Where exactly did you bury this person after you killed him?'

'In Sakura Cohen,' Kiyoshi replied, 'I can show you the exact location.'

'One point; why have you after all this time decided to tell us about it?' Nakayama enquired.

'Guilt, I couldn't live with it any longer, it's haunted me for years; gave me nightmares. I just had to tell somebody.'

'Hmmm, then let's go to the park and you can show me the spot' exclaimed the officer. He stubbed his cigarette out and rose from the chair.

Kiyoshi was going to say, "It's under the ladies' toilets," but decided against it and thought, perhaps somewhat misguidedly, that Nakayama would abandon the idea and tell him to go home. He realised that what he'd done was unorthodox but felt in the circumstances he had no choice.

'Mifune I'll need your bicycle,' Nakayama commanded.

'Isn't yours functional sir?' Mifune timidly enquired.

Kiyoshi and the Grumpy Ghost

'Of course it is, it's not for me, it's for Mr. Hirota.'

Mifune looked at Kiyoshi and then at the saddle he had moments earlier lowered.

'Raise the saddle just a couple of turns there's a good fellow we don't want Mr Hirota to get piles do we?'

Mifune didn't answer, he couldn't have cared less whether Kiyoshi contracted piles or not. He picked up the spanner and returned to the saddle that seemed to go up and down similar to the lift in the town's local department store.

'Bugger! I forgot to turn off the tape.' Nakayama returned to the interview room.

Whilst Kiyoshi waited he began to question the wisdom of his action.

"Say it was all a figment of my imagination?" He dismissed the thought; the reality of Bartholomew was something he was sure of.

"Say he had lied and there was no body beneath the ladies' conveniences?" He had confessed to a murder, even though he told police it was self-defence and assumed they would discover a body; one that forensic tests would show was several hundred years old.

"What happens if it was not found to be of a great age, or what if there was by some awful coincidence another corpse stowed away beneath the sewage pipes?"

Kiyoshi felt a twinge of panic and began to lose his nerve. Nakayama strode back into the reception area.

'All done,' he exclaimed. 'How's that bike coming on Mifune?'

'Nearly finished sir,' the pint sized constable replied with a final wrench of the spanner.

'Good, lead the way Mr. Hirota, if you would be so kind. Please take officer Mifune's bicycle and let's be on our way.'

The confession

Kiyoshi turned to the policeman, who stood poised, hands on the handlebars of his metal steed, the expression on his face denoted he would like to go as soon as possible.

'Well actually I would like to say something.'

Nakayama waited.

'Well what is it you would like to say?'

Kiyoshi hesitated, he thought of Bartholomew and the strong desire he had to be rid of him. He thought of his mother and what she would say if she found out about his confession, and the risk of disgrace he could bring to his family, and lastly he thought of Kaoru and felt a warm glow deep within.

For him to make any romantic progress with her it would be essential to be free of the ghostly presence. On the other hand, if she found out he'd confessed to a murder he could say goodbye to his dream for good.

The policemen waited. Kiyoshi was about to say something when the officers' attention was diverted by the entrance of Mr Masaguchi, a reporter for the local paper. He was a regular visitor and came in order to catch up on the local crime situation or snippets of gossip given to him by the constabulary of any interest to his readers.

'Good morning,' he stated, 'how is the world of crime and corruption in our community today?'

'It's as normal' Nakayama replied and pushed his bicycle towards the door.

'Anything unusual for my readers? Any juicy murders? Armed robbery, or scandal in the local government? Any deaths of councillors?' His questions evoked no answers.

Nakayama nodded towards Mifune.

'Look after Mr Masaguchi. Now what were you going to tell me Mr Hirota?' Masaguchi and Mifune turned and faced Kiyoshi.

Kiyoshi and the Grumpy Ghost

The trio awaited his response. Kiyoshi panicked and decided not to say anything.

'It was nothing of great importance,' he replied.

Nakayama pushed his bicycle in the direction of the door.

'Then let's be on our way.'

Kiyoshi nodded and took the handlebars of Mifune's bicycle, excused himself as he passed the reporter who regarded him with interest; a faint glimmer of recognition crept over his face.

'Excuse me, but aren't you one of the teachers at the high school in Kanmi Street?'

Kiyoshi didn't know what to say, he could hardly deny it as he had two policemen in the same room almost next to him, one with a recorded statement to say that he was. He imagined the reporter eagerly ask the vertically challenged officer as soon as he was out of earshot what was his business at the police station.

"Bloody big mouthed short arse is bound to spill everything," he thought. "It will be all over the papers."

He desperately tried to think of the best thing to do.

'My son goes to your school, perhaps you know him?' the reporter enquired.

'His name is Daiki, Daiki Masaguchi.'

Kiyoshi knew him very well, a somewhat overweight child with hardly any favourable qualities. The sort of kid that Kiyoshi disliked most, always eager to stuff his face with western-type food and emulate the American culture. Perhaps he was also biased because one thing that came out of Daiki's passion for western culture was that he watched many American films and could speak English better than Kiyoshi. Consequently, in class he would often ask awkward questions that Kiyoshi couldn't answer. He would also use the sort of language that if in less broad-minded mixed company would certainly raise a few eyebrows. Because of his youth, and a typical male of the species, he had from his interest in cinema focused more on annihilation and

The confession

destruction and the sort of films that he watched included a vocabulary from which he obtained a large amount of his knowledge. Thus it was not unusual for him to utter expletives that Kiyoshi had no knowledge of or to infer that one of his friend or associates was a person that suffered from the Oedipus complex.

He felt another bead of moisture on his brow stimulated by the thought of Masaguchi junior as he blabbed his mouth off at school.

'Er yes I think I know your son, a hard working boy, good at English,' Kiyoshi answered.

'Anyway please excuse me. I have to leave.' Kiyoshi wheeled his bicycle quickly outside; the cold air hit him as he exited. Nakayama was a short distance ahead and turned to Kiyoshi.

'Please lead on Mr Hirota.'

Kiyoshi acknowledged the policeman's request and mounted the bike. He soon pedalled head bent forward against the elements in the direction of the park.

Kiyoshi had expected a far more formal reception to his confession and not bargained for the somewhat casual response to the investigation. He somehow felt that the policeman, who swayed about on the bicycle behind him, had not taken him seriously. His expectations had led him to believe that at least, on such a day when the weather was at its most unpleasant, he would have enjoyed the comparative comfort of a patrol car to visit the "murder site".

"Must be some kind of fitness freak," thought Kiyoshi or otherwise a sadist, to inflict the discomfort of exposure to the conditions that exist inside a refrigerator.

They battled on; Kiyoshi led the way, and took it for granted that the policeman was still behind him and in a way felt insulted that his possible departure seemed to evoke no concern.

Eventually they reached the park and Nakayama pulled alongside Kiyoshi to dismount outside the ladies' toilets. It had

Kiyoshi and the Grumpy Ghost

started to snow again and Kiyoshi's chest and arms were covered with a thin powdery layer. He brushed himself down as best he could and turned to his companion.

'It's in there,' he nodded.

Nakayama displayed no outward sign of emotion or interest. After he dismounted, with as much dignity as is possible under such adverse weather conditions, he parked his bicycle against a nearby tree and strode into the interior of the ladies' loo. Kiyoshi followed. There was no chance of them encountering a member of the fair sex as the park was deserted, except for a chicken that casually pecked around on the track used for other activities rather than sustenance for hungry fowl. Kiyoshi had never seen a chicken in the park before and surmised that it must have escaped from one of the nearby gardens. It was obviously free range or at least it was now, and thought that if alone he would have attempted to pursue it and take it home where his mother would dispatch it to that chicken run in the sky then consume the remains of its earthly shell; perhaps with honey and soy sauce. Kiyoshi's gastric juices began to flow as he imagined the tender flesh dissolve in his mouth.

He was brought back to reality by the voice of Nakayama enquiring as to the whereabouts of the buried victim.

'It's here,' Kiyoshi stated and pointed his finger at the ground in front of the officer.

Nakayama looked at the concrete floor and then back to Kiyoshi.

'How are you so sure?' he asked.

'I just am, this wasn't here then, I remember that tree the one you put your bike against,' Kiyoshi continued. 'That's why I'm so certain.'

Nakayama went outside and looked at the tree to return a moment later.

'Are you sure that tree was there?' he asked.

'Positive,' Kiyoshi lied.

The confession

'How long ago was it that you said you interned the body?'

'Twenty years ago.'

'And you say that tree was here twenty years ago?'

'Er... yes, yes I'm sure it was,' Kiyoshi responded but sensed that something he had said with regard to the trees existence caused Nakayama to display a change of expression.

'Well one of my many interests in life is Bonsai and I happen to be what you could describe as intimate with the knowledge of the growth of trees, and what's more with this particular variety I have even greater rapport and I can say with a certain amount of authority sir, that that particular tree that now supports my bicycle would not have been there twenty years ago.'

Kiyoshi didn't know what to say, his credibility began to look very shaky.

"Of all the bloody bad luck I have to say the one thing that this overweight bimbo knows something about," he thought.

'There was most definitely a tree there perhaps it was cut down when they were building this place and replaced with another,' Kiyoshi responded, his credibility once more intact.

This reply seemed to satisfy the sergeant and he returned to the spot Kiyoshi had indicated.

'I'm surprised that the council didn't discover the body when they were putting them up,' Nakayama continued.

'I buried him very deep,' Kiyoshi replied, stamped his feet against the cold and breathed on his gloved hands in order to stimulate circulation, without success.

'Well, you say this is the spot and beneath here are the remains of a man you buried twenty years ago.'

'Yes,' Kiyoshi nodded.

'Right then we'll have to do a little digging to find out.'

Kiyoshi and the Grumpy Ghost

Kiyoshi breathed a mental sigh of relief and thought at least the first phase of his plan had worked. The large policeman pulled out his mobile phone from under his coat and pressed a few digits. A moment later a voice answered and Nakayama spoke.

'Who is that?' he demanded. The voice responded with a series of squeaks inaudible to Kiyoshi.

'Mrs. Ichigowa,' Nakayama boomed; he'd dialled a wrong number; growled and pressed the button required to end conversation, removed his glove, and called again, taking extra care to ensure that his chilled digits made contact with the correct numbers.

He held the phone close to his ear and listened, his breath visible as he anticipated communication with his fellow officer.

'Is that you Mifune? Right, get in touch with the local council, tell them we've got a job for them and also instruct patrol car forty-one to go back to the station, pick up some trestles and "Keep Out" signs and then make their way to the park.'

Kiyoshi shuffled around the interior of the ladies' convenience, stamped his feet and tried to keep warm. He wondered where Bartholomew was but grateful that he was not with him.

His gratitude was short lived as at the precise moment the hairy figure of his spectral colleague appeared next to Nakayama. Bartholomew looked at the policeman and then at Kiyoshi who with great restraint managed to stifle any indication he was aware that an unearthly manifestation had appeared.

'What's happening my good fellow?' Bartholomew boomed.

Kiyoshi was in a predicament. In such close proximity to Nakayama he could hardly respond to Bartholomew's question. He watched the policeman tuck the mobile phone back into his pocket and prepare to leave. Kiyoshi mouthed to his ethereal problem, the word, 'Later.' Unfortunately, Kiyoshi's pronunciation of the letter "L" came out as an "R". Bartholomew stared at the moving lips of the Japanese schoolteacher and couldn't understand what the man was trying to say.

The confession

'Speak up I can't hear you,' Bartholomew replied.

'I no can talk,' Kiyoshi blurted out and began to cough violently to distract Nakayama's attention from what he'd said.

Nakayama remained expressionless as Kiyoshi went through his fake cough routine. When the rasps had abated and his "prisoner" had regained his composure, he gestured toward the bicycle propped up against the tree outside indicating they should leave.

Kiyoshi turned to Bartholomew who had ceased his effort to elicit further conversation and stared intently at Nakayama; pulled his coat around himself and made way to the bicycle; Bartholomew followed.

The interior of the building, although somewhat draughty, had at least offered some relief from the icy wind. The large policeman instructed Kiyoshi to precede him back to the station.

They had ridden for a while heads bowed against the blast when Bartholomew drifted up alongside Kiyoshi and enquired if he was in any difficulty.

Kiyoshi could see the large mounted frame of his custodian wobble around a few yards to the rear.

'I am O.K. part of plan to get bones dug up. Please no talking with me when people

around. I can't talk back, very difficult.'

Bartholomew seemed for once to understand and nodded thoughtfully before he faded into obscurity.

Upon arrival at the police station, Kiyoshi was once more, taken into the interview room and requested to make a written statement. Mifune immediately tackled the problem of his elevated saddle whilst the sergeant again recorded Kiyoshi's confession, this time with more zeal. Perhaps the trip to the "murder spot" in the most unfavourable conditions, then stand around in the ladies' toilet convinced him of Kiyoshi's guilt.

Kiyoshi and the Grumpy Ghost

Throughout the procedure the sound of a metal spanner against a hard floor could be heard, followed by expletives as the pint sized constable endeavoured to reduce the elevation of his saddle.

After his statement had been duly recorded and signed, Kiyoshi was escorted to a holding cell at the rear of the building.

He counted on the police to find the skeleton and deduce by forensic tests that it was too old for him to have been involved in its internment. He sat in the cell and took in his surround; the inhospitable space, his imagination again took flight; images of the police being unable to find the decomposed remains danced around inside his head. He had confessed to a murder.

"But if there was no corpse then he could deny the whole thing as merely a prank. The authorities would be none too pleased but he would not be tried for murder. How long would he have to remain here?"

The prospect of having to spend more than a few hours in this confined space filled him with despair. He turned his thoughts to Kaoru and visualised himself hand in hand on a deserted beach, perhaps in Australia. Many of his friends had honeymooned there and returned with reports of beautiful beaches and hot sunny days. He sighed at the thought of such bliss. Surely a man could want for nothing more.

The temperature of the cell dropped dramatically indicating a visitor; he waited for the materialisation of Bartholomew. Nothing happened. He stood up and went to the cell door to see why the atmospheric change. A voice behind him spoke.

'Not the best of venues to spend one's time.'

Kiyoshi swung around expecting to see the scruffy form of his colleague but there was nothing only the now familiar musty smell that seemed to accompany him.

'Just thought I'd warn you I am about to appear,' the voice continued. The shape of Bartholomew materialised.

'Is that better?' he enquired, 'We were not disturbed I hope or otherwise startled?'

The confession

Kiyoshi was puzzled by the use of the word "we" but understood Bartholomew's meaning.

'No I no startled, better for me.'

'Well, may I ask what you are doing here?' Bartholomew enquired, pulled up the tails of his tattered coat and sat himself next to Kiyoshi.

Kiyoshi regarded his new cellmate and wondered why he sat. Surely he had no gravitational pull to contend with.

'Why you sit down?' Kiyoshi asked.

'I beg your pardon?'

'Why you sit down? You no get tired, do you?'

'Have you any objection to my being seated?' Bartholomew responded, a hint of indignation in his voice.

'No, I like if you like to sit down. I just wondering why you want to sit down and if you get tired?'

'If you must know it's habit; I do things that I have done all my life. Well whilst I was alive let me say. But enough of this, what is the current situation at present concerning the remnants of my mortal coil?'

'Huh?' Kiyoshi understood two thirds of what Bartholomew had said but comprehended the gist of his cell mate's statement. His utterance gave him time to think of a response and perhaps of the chance to hear it again.

'Sir, you are a teacher of the English language your grasp of the aforementioned is pathetic. I repeat, what is the situation concerning my bones, my body the remnants of the item of which I spoke at length when I first asked for your assistance? The very reason I sought your help.'

Kiyoshi felt his pulse quicken. He had never professed to be a fluent speaker of English; he was merely a teacher at the local school and been lumbered with the English language course because he studied English at University as a second subject.

Kiyoshi and the Grumpy Ghost

He had a grasp of the language if the speaker spoke slowly and clearly and felt that he most certainly did not deserve the scorn of another for his shortcomings. Besides the person, or entity to put it correctly, spoke in a manner that was none too easy to understand and he'd gone to a great deal of trouble to help him.

'Why you say bad things to me?' Kiyoshi stated and cared not if Bartholomew was a ghost.

'Why you no speak Japanese? You say you here four hundred month, er I mean year, and you cannot speak, what you been doing all time? I here now because of you, I say I murder some person so you get bones. Police dig up for us but big chance for me to get trouble. I trust you. How I know bones there; I tell police I kill some person, that terrible thing.'

Bartholomew regarded the irate man at length before he spoke.

'To answer your first question, I cannot speak your language because I have never learned it. I was killed before I had the chance, and yes I have been here for some considerable time but lived in a different dimension awaiting the right opportunity to cross into yours.

You are the first person I have conversed with for nearly four hundred years. Time for you will pass, change your appearance, but for me it has been a period of existence without existing; I don't expect you to understand what I am saying and hope you never experience the same condition. As to your other statement about your confession to a murder in order to facilitate the removal of my bones; I can only say that I am sorry if I insulted you and I appreciate your effort on my behalf.'

Kiyoshi remained silent while he tried to work out Bartholomew's words; he came to the conclusion that he had received an apology.

'So O.K. many things I no understand but maybe I not want to,' he replied. 'I only know there is thing that I never believe before and because of this my whole life change.'

The confession

Beneath his hair covered face, a slight flicker of a smile played upon the lips of Bartholomew.

'Very well then sir, now what?' he enquired.

'I stay here until they find body very old and I no murderer.'

'But what will the authorities do with them?' Bartholomew asked.

'I ask for bones and say because of trouble I bury at own expense.'

'I hope they are as forthcoming as you say.'

'Force?' Kiyoshi repeated.

'As helpful as you believe,' Bartholomew said without any hint of patronisation.

'I hope too.'

'Is there anything I can get you?' Bartholomew asked. 'Anything you need at all?'

Kiyoshi was taken by surprise by Bartholomew's offer. The whole time that he'd known him he'd always made demands and never enquired as to the welfare or well-being of his potential saviour.

'It O.K.' he replied. 'I want get out of this place.'

'Any time you want just say so,' Bartholomew responded. There was the sound of a turned lock and the cell door swung open. Kiyoshi waited for a face to appear at the entrance but none materialised.

'You do that?' he asked in amazement.

'If I can transport you from one place to another then the mere opening of a door is but nothing.'

Kiyoshi remembered the "flying" incident in front of the Yakitori seller and felt ashamed that he had forgotten; although it was because of Bartholomew that he'd been there in the first place.

'I stay here until prove I innocent.'

'Of course, but it is always of a pleasant flavour to know that there is an exit if required. Are you sure there is nothing else I can do for you?'

Kiyoshi's opinion of Bartholomew began to change from fear and obligation to one who had discovered a fairy Godmother.

'No, I sure. How I contact you to speak?'

Kiyoshi enquired and sensed that his ethereal friend was about to vanish.

'I will be back, do not concern yourself, I will know if you want to talk with me.'

Bartholomew faded along with the musty aroma Kiyoshi had become accustomed to, so much so he hadn't noticed it.

With the departure of Bartholomew, Kiyoshi had time to reflect upon his circumstances, he looked at the four walls around him; the prospect of several years incarceration in such a small space was more than he could bear. He glanced at the half open door and wondered what the reaction would be when it was discovered he could have had access to the outside at any time. No doubt there would be a few red faces.

CHAPTER 4

Freedom at a price

He heard the voice of Mifune, the door opened. The expression on the face at the doorway changed from one of horror, to relief and then to puzzlement. It was as if he was an actor instructed by the director to portray emotions by the use of facial contortions when he entered a room.

Kiyoshi however, thought Mifune's entrance although dramatic, amusing, and unquestionably the unlocked door would go no further as it was Mifune himself who escorted Kiyoshi to the cell and locked it.

Mifune recovered his composure and addressed his charge.

'Do you want a drink?' he enquired.

'Yes, that would be nice thank you, anything to break the monotony. And could I have something to read, if it's not too much trouble?'

Mifune nodded and closed the door. Kiyoshi heard the key turn and the door tried twice before the vertically handicapped policeman was satisfied it was locked and the prisoner secure.

Meanwhile back at the park in the building where the remains of Bartholomew had been interned; the area was cordoned off and the sound of a pneumatic drill audible to those people who had the misfortune to live within close proximity.

Eventually the clatter of the machine ceased and the tremors in the earth under the relentless repetitive stab of the steel dagger stopped as the concrete gave way to the softer soil.

Kiyoshi and the Grumpy Ghost

Nakayama peered into the hole and nodded approvingly. It was late and he was hungry, but he was a punctilious police officer and felt obliged to remain on site until satisfied that every effort had been made to find a corpse in the place indicated by the suspect.

'Right we'll use shovels now and please be careful we don't want to destroy any evidence.'

He used the term "we" but did not include himself in the group of persons involved in the actual dig. A gang of four labourers had been contracted for the task of the exhumation and due to receive a handsome remuneration for their effort.

The light outside faded and added one more element of discomfort as the temperature fell. The wind dropped and it started to snow again. Large flakes floated earthward. Nakayama stood in the entrance of the building and watched their descent made visible by the light of a lamp post a few yards from him; he fumbled in his pocket for his cigarettes. In the summer, he thought, that same lamp post would be surrounded by the fluttering wings of hundreds of insects perhaps equal to the amount of snowflakes that he now could see fall through the light cast by the lamp.

Bartholomew reappeared in Kiyoshi's cell his posture upright, his shoulders thrown back. He thumped the small oriental on the back in a gesture of eager anticipation of his departure once and for all from his earthly bondage. Kiyoshi reeled under the impact and tottered forward. He quickly regained composure, forced a smile at the benevolent ghost and nodded his head.

'Good news,' Bartholomew beamed. 'They have unearthed my mortal remains.'

'Good news,' Kiyoshi repeated and thought to himself that indeed it was good news if only to be spared such outbursts.

'This is a fortunate day for me and my heartfelt thanks to you, sir,' Bartholomew took hold of Kiyoshi's hand and shook it vigorously. The reverberation from the ethereal pump travelled up and down Kiyoshi's arm.

Freedom at a price

The hand felt cold but the grip was strong and Kiyoshi's spine tingled at the realisation of what had transpired. He had mostly overcome his fear of his visitor from the other side but such intimate contact still caused him to feel apprehensive.

'I am indeed grateful to you, sir,' Bartholomew continued and let go his grasp.

'Now hope that can be buried,' Kiyoshi stated.

'Yes indeed, and for you to continue with your life.'

'I see they have locked the door again; do you want to leave this place?'

'No I will wait and see policeman.'

'Policeman,' Bartholomew spoke the word slowly, not too familiar with it.

'As you wish but I will at least give you the choice.'

Once again Kiyoshi heard the sound of a lock turn and the cell door swung slowly open.

'Maybe better if door still locked,' Kiyoshi said.

'Balderdash!' Bartholomew bellowed. 'I like not the idea of my friend being interned against his will with no access to his freedom. I shall return.' His image faded from view.

Kiyoshi stood in the open doorway and contemplated the consequences of such a situation. It would not look too good. But there again it could not be construed as his fault. He had made no attempt to escape and how could he possibly open the door from the inside.

Kiyoshi remained in his cell and read the magazine Mifune had brought him earlier. He felt hungry, his appetite returned upon the news of the discovery. His mind worked out what to say to the police in respect as to how he knew the existence of the corpse.

The sound of footsteps grew louder and then an intake of breath before two pairs of feet increased their pace from a walk into a run. Once again the door burst open and this time

Nakayama stood framed in the doorway; behind him the somewhat smaller shape of Mifune peered intently under his arm in order to ascertain whether Kiyoshi was still in the cell.

Nakayama turned to Mifune, his countenance visibly darkened as his glance of disdain at Mifune's negligence bored into the small officer whose stature seemed to diminish even further.

'What is the meaning of leaving the door unlocked?' he said, an underlying tone of menace in his voice.

'I locked it. I'm sure I did sir.'

Kiyoshi, whilst not exactly a lover of Mifune, had no particular dislike of him and after all he had lent him his bicycle.

'The lock is faulty I think,' Kiyoshi said.

'It just clicked open about ten minutes after Officer Mifune closed it.'

Nakayama bent down and examined the lock. There was nothing that he could see from the outside even if the lock was at fault. Nakayama behaved rather like those persons who know nothing about cars and if buying, kick the tyres as part of their inspection process.

'Hmmm,' Nakayama muttered.

'Give me the key Mifune,' he demanded, still not convinced.

Mifune handed it over.

'Now go inside and I'll lock the door from the outside.'

Kiyoshi watched with some amusement as the two police officers puzzled the situation.

"He could hardly lock it from the inside," he thought.

Nakayama thrust the key into the lock and methodically turned it, withdrew it and pressed his weight against the door. If anything would prove the weakness of the security system it would be the sizeable bulk of Nakayama hurled against it, like an indignant rhino enraged by the presence of a vehicle on its territory. Visions of hippopotami and elephants also came to Kiyoshi's mind as Nakayama continued to thud against the door.

The door unlocked and the "rhino" re-appeared, flushed by his effort to prove that the lock was perfectly sound and clearly his subordinate officer's negligence was responsible for the security lax.

Nakayama said nothing but adopted an expression of smugness mixed with contempt, elevated his nose an inch or two and turned to Kiyoshi.

'Sir we have found the remains of the person that you allegedly murdered and they have been taken to the forensic laboratory. You will be held overnight and officially charged in the morning. Is there anything that you would like to say in relation to this matter?'

'There is just one thing,' Kiyoshi took a deep breath.

'And what may that be?'

'I didn't murder anyone.'

Nakayama exchanged a quick glance with his fellow officer.

'I see, and what has brought about this change of heart? Perhaps you could tell me who it is that we have exhumed in the park and how you knew it was there?'

'The remains of the person in the park belong to a sailor who was murdered by his fellow seaman nearly four hundred years ago.'

Again Nakayama shot a glance to Mifune who listened with interest to Kiyoshi's statement.

'And, if I might ask, how do you know this?'

'It was a dream I had,' Kiyoshi continued, to keep the truth of Bartholomew's visitation out of it.

'A dream?' Nakayama reiterated.

'Yes, I could hardly come into the police station and say that I had a dream about a body buried in a certain spot. I don't think you would have acted upon such information.'

'You are certainly right there, sir,' the burly policeman replied.

'Well then I suggest that you get some sleep and we will see you in the morning and discuss this matter further when we have some results from forensics. If what you say has any element of truth, it is still a serious matter using the resources of the establishment to authenticate the validity of your imagination.'

Kiyoshi said nothing; Nakayama wore a disgruntled expression, Mifune one of interest as they left the cell.

He returned to his bunk and tried to make himself comfortable. After tossing and turning for most of the night, he eventually fell asleep.

The raucous call of a crow outside his cell heralded the dawn and woke him from sleep; momentarily confused as to his whereabouts, the realisation came to him as he took in the stark walls of his cell. He felt stiff around the upper back and neck and rotated his head in a circular movement to try and alleviate the discomfort.

The door unlocked; he was unsure whether it was Bartholomew's work or the police. It was Mifune; he carried a bowl of rice and Miso soup. A raw egg wobbled on top of the rice. Even in such conditions and under the circumstances he now found himself, he could not prevent his mind from comparing the movement of the egg yolk to that of his beloved's breast.

Mifune placed the tray down and handed him a copy of the morning paper.

The vertically challenged police officer could no longer contain his curiosity and casually said, 'So tell me more about this dream then.'

Kiyoshi looked at the officer and then back to the tray of food.

Freedom at a price

'Dream?' he repeated and thought hard to remember what he had dreamt, if anything, in the night.

'Yes dream, you said you dreamt about the body buried in the park. What kind of dream was it, a clear vision, or a voice that came to you?' Mifune enquired.

'Oh, that dream,' Kiyoshi clawed back his senses from their night's inactivity.

'Well, it was er, more a voice telling me, it was in English and at first I found it difficult to understand.'

'Fascinating,' Mifune stated, his mouth agape.

Kiyoshi thought that not only was he extremely small but he also looked like a tortoise. He resigned himself not to complain about his own appearance in future and be thankful that he was not Mifune who seemed to have been given a nasty smack with the ugly stick and at the back of the queue when physical attributes were handed out.

"At least the man believes me," Kiyoshi mused.

'Please tell me more I'm extremely interested in phenomena of this kind and read many books on the subject.'

Kiyoshi was surprised that there were any books on the subject but nodded all the same. He glanced at the soup and suspected that it was on its way to cold.

Mifune noticed his interest in the tray.

'Please eat,' he requested and gestured toward the food.

'Thank you, I will,' Kiyoshi reached over to the tray. 'When will you get the results from forensics?'

'Should be sometime this morning,' Mifune answered.

Kiyoshi nodded and dipped his chopsticks into the bowl of Miso soup. He was about to place a particularly appetising piece of tofu extracted from the hot liquid, into his mouth, when the headlines of the paper caught his eye. What he read caused him to instantly lose any desire for nourishment.

Kiyoshi and the Grumpy Ghost

"SCHOOL TEACHER CONFESSES TO MURDER"

He dropped the chopsticks, replaced the bowl and grabbed the newspaper in one swift movement.

He felt a cold sweat break out followed by a hot flush and then a tingle that ran through the remnants of hair that sprouted from his scalp.

'Well thank you very much!' Kiyoshi growled as he scanned the article and searched for mention of his name.

Mifune regarded the schoolteacher as he read.

'It doesn't give your name.'

'It doesn't have to,' Kiyoshi snapped back.

'It gives the name of the school, my description and the subject I teach. Why did you tell that reporter about me?'

'With all due respect Mr Hirota, you came into the police station and confessed to a murder, a very serious offence. What do you expect?'

Kiyoshi knew the man was right but couldn't help feel hostility toward the reporter for complicating his life even more.

'Why did you tell him?' Kiyoshi asked.

'Why shouldn't I?' Mifune responded.

'If you had told the truth in the first place you would not be in this situation.'

'If I had told the truth you wouldn't have believed me,' Kiyoshi countered.

'I'm sure we would have done something,' Mifune replied.

'Do you believe me?' Kiyoshi enquired.

'Well let's say I don't disbelieve you. How else could you have known those remains were buried there?'

Kiyoshi looked at the open newspaper on his lap.

'But this, this is terrible, people will believe I'm a murderer.'

'I repeat, if you go into a police station and make a statement to that effect what can you expect?'

'But I assumed that it would not be reported until the remains had been found and I had been cleared of any suspicion.'

'Well all I can say is that you were wrong to make such an assumption. If it will make you feel better, I will contact the reporter and inform him of further developments once we have forensic results.'

It didn't make him feel any better. The damage had been done. If Kaoru had read this, which no doubt she had, then he could say goodbye to any thoughts of a future relationship and also to his job. Such a scandal now public knowledge could not be tolerated, his contract terminated.

Even his mother would frown on such a thing. She had tolerated her son's unconventional behaviour over the years but murder was well over the top.

The sound of Nakayama's voice penetrated the cell beckoning his subordinate to come to the reception area. Mifune bowed to Kiyoshi and exited, checked the lock, then departed to answer the summons of his superior.

Kiyoshi sat immersed in gloom to stare at the newspaper headlines.

Perhaps it wasn't such a good idea after all. If he had never encountered that obnoxious spirit, he wouldn't have been in this predicament. His life would have stayed well within his comfort zone and he could have plodded along in his daily routine with no stress other than the normal trials endured by Japanese school teachers which due to his years of experience he'd reduced to a minimum. The newspaper fell to the floor. Kiyoshi sank forward his head in his hands, all thought of food gone from his mind.

Three hours later the door of the cell opened and Nakayama entered. Kiyoshi had noticed movement throughout the morning, heard voices from the reception area, and listened for any news.

Kiyoshi and the Grumpy Ghost

He stood up as the policeman came in. Nakayama's bulk made the cell seem even smaller. Kiyoshi searched his face.

"Had he had word from forensics?"

The portly Japanese Peeler stared at him without a word.

'Well?' Kiyoshi asked.

'Have you heard anything?'

Nakayama slowly nodded.

'Please come this way.' He indicated to Kiyoshi to leave the cell.

Kiyoshi contained his enthusiasm to express relief and walked ahead of Nakayama through the open door to the reception area, then into the interview room.

'Please be seated,' Nakayama requested.

Kiyoshi did as he was asked.

The police officer started the tape to record procedure, adjusted his chair and reached in his pocket for his cigarettes. He offered one to Kiyoshi who shook his head.

'No thank you.'

Nakayama went through the preliminary vocal requirements necessary to establish time and date of interview. He lit his cigarette, snapped shut his Zippo and inhaled a lung full of nicotine laden smoke.

'Right then, Mr Hirota,' Nakayama's attitude was far less amiable than on their first encounter.

Kiyoshi was puzzled. Surely if proven that he was not a criminal then his reception should be more hospitable, not the opposite.

'So how did you know human remains were located where you indicated?

'I had a dream, a kind of vision,' Kiyoshi replied.

Freedom at a price

Nakayama did a double take, readjusted his stoic expression and continued.

'When did you actually have this dream?'

'It was about a week ago,' Kiyoshi lied.

'I had it over a period of three nights and then I came to you.'

'You had the same dream on three separate occasions?'

'Yes, the first night I took no notice only that it was vivid. The second night I was more surprised than anything else, and on the third night convinced that it was some kind of communication, a message.'

Nakayama betrayed no emotion as he listened to Kiyoshi.

'You have obviously verified my story then?' Kiyoshi enquired earnestly.

'We found that the bones are of considerable age, probably three or four hundred years old.'

Kiyoshi breathed a sigh of relief.

'Does that mean I am free to go?'

'I can't hold you. You have retracted your previous statement and the age of the bones verifies that you could not have been the cause of the internment.'

'Well that's a relief,' Kiyoshi stated.

'I er realise that I have caused you a bit of bother and what I would like to propose is that to save you any further inconvenience I'll re-bury the remains, at my own expense of course, at some other location.'

Kiyoshi realised as he spoke, his request in the face of a bureaucracy that seldom demonstrated flexibility, would be denied. When he first formulated the plan it didn't seem unreasonable but as his tongue formed the last consonants of his sentence, the thought struck him that what he asked had less chance of fulfilment than finding a fart in a Jacuzzi.

Kiyoshi and the Grumpy Ghost

Nakayama's face twitched and the faint glimmer of a smile forced the corners of his mouth to extend in an upward direction for a split second. Kiyoshi emulated the officer's amusement and was left with teeth exposed long after Nakayama's face had resumed its normal expression; the policeman's beady eyes stared blankly across at him.

'Mr Hirota, how you came to know the whereabouts of the skeleton is, I must confess, a puzzle and I have a suspicion that there is more to this than meets the eye. We have gone to a considerable amount of trouble and expense to excavate this historical find and we certainly will not hand it over to you so that you may re-bury it. It will be given to the appropriate authorities and taken to Tokyo. There is also the matter of a false statement to the police, which in itself carries a severe penalty.'

Kiyoshi felt the first twinge of anxiety as he looked at the policeman who obviously enjoyed the moment.

The words "severe penalty" echoed in his brain, visions of courtrooms, bespectacled officials and shuffling papers.

'But I had no choice; if I told you I had a dream would you have gone to the trouble to dig up the remains?'

Nakayama's face softened.

'Of course I realise that you had no choice, you must also realise that we have no choice in this matter. There is perhaps one solution to this dilemma that we could look at.'

'What's that?' Kiyoshi remarked eager to hear any suggestion that could get him off the hook.

'If you were prepared to meet the cost of the work done in regard to the excavation, then obviously we would be most appreciative and consider the matter in a more favourable light.'

Kiyoshi realised that it was blackmail but could do nothing about it. It also would turn out to be bloody expensive, contract workers charge like wounded bulls at the normal rate. A team of

Freedom at a price

them who'd worked overtime for several hours would be like a stampede of irate bovine flesh stampeding toward him, all badly hurt, seeking retribution; indeed, a financial burden he didn't know whether he could afford. The alternative seemed worse. Kiyoshi mentally cursed Bartholomew.

"It was his entire fault. Why did he let himself in for all this?"

'How much are we actually looking at?' Kiyoshi asked.

'We'll send you a bill Mr Hirota.'

'Thank you you're most kind.' Kiyoshi inclined his head in a bow.

The policeman responded in like manner and the two men rose from the table.

'You are free to go.'

Kiyoshi bowed once more and followed Nakayama into the reception area.

'Give Mr Hirota his belongings; his things are in the cupboard,' Nakayama instructed. Mifune was deeply engrossed in conversation with Masaguchi the reporter responsible for the headlines.

Kiyoshi caught sight of the newshound and realised he was about to face the consequences of his actions. As far as the local population was concerned he was a murderer. He felt another flush of anxiety sweep over him, the follicles on his head tingled as small beads of perspiration formed on his sparsely foliated scalp. Masaguchi and Mifune ceased their conversation as he and Nakayama entered the reception area.

'Mr Hirota, could I possibly have a few words with you?'

Kiyoshi was anxious to speak to the reporter to put the record straight and to clear his name.

'I understand that you have retracted your statement?' Masaguchi enquired.

'Yes, I am not a murderer as your paper states.'

'Our paper makes no such accusation Mr Hirota, it merely says the facts. That a school teacher confessed to a murder, now I am given to understand that the skeleton found is several hundred years old. Can you explain this?'

'I would like your paper to publish the fact that I am not a murderer and that I invented the story because I was continually haunted by a dream.'

Mifune appeared with Kiyoshi's coat and belongings.

'Would you please sign here?' He pointed to a piece of paper produced from one of the drawers in the reception desk.

Kiyoshi picked up the pen scribbled his signature, pocketed his few belongings and proceeded to dress himself in preparation for his encounter with the elements.

'Mr. Hirota,' Masaguchi repeated. 'Can you please elaborate?'

Kiyoshi, satisfied that his attire would offer him sufficient protection, turned toward the inquisitive face of the reporter. It crossed Kiyoshi's mind he resembled his unfortunate offspring. He shuddered at the thought of glee his progeny would manifest at their next encounter, armed with the knowledge his father would impart to him, if he had not already done so, although by now the whole village would know.

'I would like to make it perfectly clear that I did not murder anyone.'

'Then why did you say that you did?' interrupted the reporter.

'If you'd kindly let me finish, I had a recurring dream and... er... heard this voice distinctly tell me to confess to a crime, in order to facilitate the removal of the skeleton, that has lain beneath the earth for over four hundred years.'

Masaguchi scribbled in a notebook as Kiyoshi spoke.

'Please continue.'

'There is nothing more to say,' replied Kiyoshi somewhat curtly.

Freedom at a price

'So please make sure that you tell your readers that I am innocent of any crime.'

'What was the dream about and the voice, tell me more about the voice what did it actually say?'

Kiyoshi had invented the voice to make the story sound more plausible and in a strange way to ease his conscience by a half-truth. He wished he had just left it at a dream.

'It said,' Kiyoshi tried desperately to think of something Bartholomew uttered relevant to the situation, 'that I was to help.'

'How many times did you have this dream and when did the voice speak to you?'

'I had the dream six times.'

'Every night for six days?' The reporter asked.

'It was over a three-week period.'

The problem with lies, unlike the truth, is it's difficult to recollect what you have said; Kiyoshi decided he would in future make a mental effort to remember what he'd said to enforce his past statements. It was fortunate that Nakayama was not within earshot when he related the recently changed facts, to dispute them.

"What did I say to the rhino?" Kiyoshi tried to recall.

'What, twice a week?' Masaguchi continued.

'Is it really important?' Kiyoshi retorted.

'I mean does it really matter when I had them?'

Masaguchi continued to write in his notebook and ignored the hint of irritation in Kiyoshi's voice.

He ceased to write and regarded Kiyoshi with an unfriendly stare.

'Mr Hirota, if you want me to put the record straight and clear your name, I would suggest you answer my questions and allow me to do just that.'

Kiyoshi and the Grumpy Ghost

Kiyoshi turned to the reporter who wore the same inane expression he shared with his son. This time a trace of something in Masaguchi's features told Kiyoshi he had him over a barrel and he'd better be more cooperative, answer the questions or his journalistic reprieve would not happen.

"Another bloody blackmailer," thought Kiyoshi. He took a deep breath to help organise his response.

'I told you, I had the dream over a period of weeks.' Kiyoshi related the story as told to Nakayama. 'It was only when it recurred three days on the trot that I took notice.'

'When was that?' Masaguchi asked.

'Last week,' Kiyoshi lied. 'If you would forgive me I have a few things to do.' Kiyoshi pulled his coat around him and made toward the door.

Masaguchi stepped aside. 'I might call you later to verify a few things. Is that all right with you Mr Hirota?'

'Yes of course,' Kiyoshi answered.

The weather had improved; Kiyoshi descended the steps of the police station and on to the snow covered pavement; his shoes crunched on the crisp layer of frozen water. At least he was a free man.

On his way home he thought about his position and what lay ahead.

To all, he was at this moment, a suspected murderer, a criminal and imagined his life would be a challenge until the newspaper article cleared him. He had misgivings to begin with about confessing to a crime, but now that the article was public his worst fears had come into fruition with a vengeance. He wondered what had become of Bartholomew and the course of action he would follow now that the bones were out of his hands.

"I can do bugger all," he mused. "The authorities certainly won't give them back to me."

CHAPTER 5

The consequences

The journey home was uneventful and those persons he encountered showed no sign of recognition of a cold blooded killer.

His mother was in the garden and made use of the watery winter sun to dry recently washed clothes. Kiyoshi breezed in as though nothing had happened. He acknowledged his mother with a nod and went inside to the warmth of the house. The cat cleaned itself in the front room, its left hind leg raised as it meticulously moved its rough tongue up and down the length of its tail. It stopped its ablutions as Kiyoshi entered and regarded him in a nervous fashion as if to expect the ethereal shape of Bartholomew to materialise.

He removed his shoes and outer garments and patted Kuro on the head as he passed. His nostrils were assailed by the smell of food that simmered on the stove; his empty stomach reacted. The aroma began to increase the flow of gastric juices as he made his way to the kitchen.

He was about to lift the lid of a pot of miso soup when his mother returned from the garden with an empty washing basket. She stood still and stared at her son but spoke not a word. Kiyoshi felt uncomfortable under the intensity of her gaze and pretended to be interested in the bowl of miso.

At last she broke her silence.

'There was a message for you from the head master.'

'Oh really,' Kiyoshi responded in an attempt to appear as casual as possible; he wondered what knowledge his mother had of recent events. 'What did he want?' He waited for the bombshell.

'He said for you not to bother to attend when the staff meets prior to the start of term.'

'Oh I wonder why not?' Kiyoshi feigned surprise.

'Perhaps he thought that you had been there long enough to know all the procedures. Or maybe that you needed an extra day's holiday, or it could be, although I hardly imagine, it had something to do with you murdering somebody. But I doubt if he would worry about such a trivial thing. I really couldn't say.'

Kiyoshi remained quiet and tried to formulate an explanation to give his mother. What could he say? There was silence except for the gentle bubble from a pot of nabe, a nutritious dish of vegetables, seafood and meat, a favourite among Sumo wrestlers.

The smell of the miso wafted up from the pot and mingled with the hot nabe. Kiyoshi's mind was for a second diverted by the joint aroma of the two dishes.

'I can explain,' he stammered.

'Remember I told you about the ghost and I asked you if someone helped me then would I be obligated to help them and you....'

Kiyoshi stopped. His mother wore an expression that he'd seen many times before, an expression that clearly told him he shouldn't waste his breath and she'd already made up her mind not to believe it.

'All right what if I said that I had a dream, the same dream several nights and that in the dream there were the remains of a man buried under the ladies' toilet in the park and I was chosen to be instrumental in their recovery. What would you say?'

The consequences

His mother narrowed her eyes as if her thought processes were working overtime.

'I wouldn't say anything,' she retorted.

Kiyoshi had already taken a breath in order to defend himself against the tirade that he expected to follow but was taken aback by his mother's reply.

'You wouldn't say anything?' he tentatively asked.

'Nothing,' his mother responded.

'Why not?'

'What would be the point you are not going to tell me, all this talk of ghosts and dreams. I've given up with you, for years I've been saying that you should get a wife, get married settle down, have a family and all the time you have had no intention of complying with my wishes. I've introduced you to several girls from good backgrounds and you've refused them all, choosing to pine over some Korean girl. Well after this I don't suppose even she will want to know you. So why should I care?'

'You don't believe that I actually murdered someone do you? There'll be an explanation in tomorrow's paper clearing me of any guilt. Why do you think they released me? You don't think they'd let me go if they thought I was guilty'.

His mother glared at her son.

'I rang the police station and spoke to an officer and he told me you had been released.'

'So you know that I didn't do it.'

'I know that you are a fool, obstinate, pig headed like your father and completely selfish, but not a murderer. Why you did this thing I don't know, no doubt you had your reasons but you must now face the consequences of your actions and don't look to me for help.'

His mother pushed past him and returned to her cooking. Kiyoshi watched her leave, her grey hair tied in a loose bun and a mole on the base of her neck she'd had as long as he could remember. He felt for a second or two a pang of guilt that he didn't share with her more details of the intimate side of his life, but soon dismissed it as ridiculous and knew that his mother would strongly disapprove of most of his shenanigans, and those that she was aware of would impart to her friend Mrs Ishida; who in turn would tell the community at large.

Kiyoshi left the kitchen and entered the living room, a newspaper was on top of the kotatsu but he showed no interest. He kneeled down, thrust his legs under the skirt of the table and pondered his situation.

Since Bartholomew's appearance he had experienced nothing but aggravation of one sort or another, and now to cap it all he had no job. How could he possibly pay the bill for the excavation? He knew as sure as eggs were eggs he would receive one. A sense of dejection crept over him, the one thought that gave him any sense of pleasure was that of Kaoru but this soon turned to dismay as he imagined her reaction to the newspaper article that depicted him as a murderer.

There was a distinct smell of musk and then, to Kiyoshi, the unmistakable sound of Bartholomew's voice.

'Sir, I am in need of your assistance once again. I don't have much time.'

Kiyoshi watched the figure of the spectre materialise. A few days ago he would have quivered with fear, a mass of loose bowels then faint, but now no such reaction. His response was to wait almost impatiently as Bartholomew's image became clearer.

'You. You make life very hard. I help.' In his excited state Kiyoshi found it even more difficult to form the words that his emotions demanded.

'I have no job, I to pay men for digging, I very upset,' he continued, and glared at Bartholomew.

'My dear sir please calm yourself and listen, it is vital that you understand what I am saying,' Bartholomew announced in a clear loud voice that caused Kiyoshi to stop in mid-sentence;

The consequences

not because of the volume and authority contained in the apparition's voice, but the sheer audacity that Bartholomew demonstrated by a request for him to remain silent and demand he give him further help.

'They are removing my mortal remains.'

'Eh?' responded Kiyoshi, a look of bewilderment on his face.

'They are taking my bones away, removing them,' Bartholomew stated in a calm voice.

'I think that what you want,' Kiyoshi replied.

'Of course not, you buffoon!' Bartholomew boomed, calm no longer.

Kiyoshi gaped at the hirsute face of his ethereal tormentor and said nothing.

'If my remains are taken from this spot then I have to follow. I can feel myself getting weaker. They are moving away even as I speak.'

Kiyoshi's mind translated and unravelled the facts that Bartholomew had presented.

'You mean, you go where bones go?'

'Exactly, once I have made a connection with them I must be within a certain radius or I will lose my chance of peace.'

'What I do?' Kiyoshi retorted.

'How can help?'

'But you must help, you are my last chance.'

'Someone else help,' Kiyoshi replied smugly.

'But they can't, I can only request the help of two persons,' Bartholomew pleaded. 'Sir, I beg of you please take pity, please don't withdraw your aid. I am indeed eternally grateful for your help thus far and will always be greatly indebted to you.'

Kiyoshi and the Grumpy Ghost

Bartholomew dropped to one knee to come level with the seated Kiyoshi, his large bearded face inches away. His expression wore a look of anguish that Kiyoshi hadn't seen before.

Kiyoshi mulled over the rules of the supernatural, who actually said that he could only ask two people?

The figure of his mother appeared at the entrance to the living room. She was confronted by the sight of her son as he stared into space and spoke in a foreign tongue. This in itself was not unusual as she had witnessed this phenomenon often over the last few days but it was the glazed look in her son's eyes that caused her to raise her eyebrows, shake her head in despair and return to her chores.

The mental process that had caused Kiyoshi to stare with such inanity into space was motivated by the single thought that Bartholomew was in a situation that forced him to depart whether he wanted to or not. He would finally be free. He regarded the features of his spirit companion contorted in distress even though a large part of his face was obscured by hair. He remained unmoved.

This apparition, this visitation this manifestation from another dimension had caused him a great deal of bother. Let him experience the obnoxious taste of his own medicine.

Kiyoshi feigned a troubled look.

'I'm sorry there is nothing can do to help.'

Bartholomew stood up his head downcast and shoulders drooped, his very spiritual essence depleted.

'Then sir, I thank you and bid you farewell.'

The last image that Kiyoshi saw of Bartholomew was that of a dejected figure in the middle of his living room fade into obscurity.

Kiyoshi took in the full implication of his companion's departure. He was free. He no longer had obligations of the ethereal kind. He was free to continue, to carry on his mundane existence without any interference from the spirit world. He had become quite blasé in the last day or two in regard to the existence of ghostly forms and used to the idea that there was a life beyond the grave though he didn't understand the rules. His own situation loomed into his mind.

What was he to do? He would go to the school first thing tomorrow and explain, armed with the retraction of the implication of guilt of any crime, other than false statement in regard to homicide. He felt sure he would regain the position he'd held for years in which he had diligently performed his duties in the education of a bunch of little monsters that had no desire to learn.

Kiyoshi remained, legs outstretched under the skirts of the heated table, as his mind sought to arrange the sequence of events that had transpired over the last few days. The myriad of images and thoughts, together with the change of emotion that each recounted event stimulated, proved too much for the schoolteacher; he slipped into a dreamlike state where fantasy and reality blend into one.

He awoke the next morning in the same position brought back to the conscious state by a vivid dream that he was in an old deserted mine shaft and there had been a "cave in". The sheer weight of the massive stone and timber crashed down on his chest to push the last gasp of air from his broken body. He began to gasp for breath and opened his eyes. As his lids prized themselves apart the first thing he saw was an enormous feline face inches from his own. The big yellow eyes half closed in a kind of catlike euphoria as it sucked up the warmth from the human's body beneath; it purred, and saliva from its mouth dribbled in small droplets onto his chin. Kiyoshi sat up and pushed the cat away. The rotund creature stepped lightly off his "hot water bottle" shook his corpulent body and with all the dignity that one so obese can muster, raised his tail and strutted off in the direction of the kitchen.

"I must have fallen asleep. Why didn't mother wake me up? What time is it?"

Kiyoshi and the Grumpy Ghost

He withdrew his legs from the table and raised himself from the floor. He had a sensation of stiffness in his neck and turned his head first in one direction then the other, at the same time rubbed the base of his skull with a cramped right hand; he gave a loud sigh and went to the kitchen to find out the time. It was nine thirty in the morning and his stomach rumbled; he hadn't eaten for several hours. He couldn't remember the exact time that he fell asleep but knew it was some time ago.

His mother was nowhere to be seen. There was warm rice in the rice cooker; Kiyoshi helped himself to a bowl, he was one of those men who lacked culinary skills and would probably die of malnutrition if left to his own devices for more than three weeks.

His immediate hunger pangs abated, he hastily showered, got dressed and hurried to the nearest newspaper vendor. He entered the shop and looked at the man behind the counter to calculate the reaction to his presence; there was none. Kiyoshi took the paper and hurried back to his home. He resisted the temptation to stop and peruse it in the street, the weather had turned even colder and the recently fallen snow a sheet of ice.

Arriving at his house he let himself in. The cat was in the centre of the living room cleaning itself again as Kiyoshi changed his shoes, threw off his coat and tossed it into the nearest chair. Kuro promptly jumped onto the dishevelled piece of material, padded the cloth with his forepaws to rearrange it into a more comfortable shape then settled down. The garment still exuded some of Kiyoshi's bodily warmth and the animal lowered its furry form into the folds of the coat with a contented purr. Kiyoshi was far too absorbed in the paper to take any notice of the cats sleeping arrangements even if it did involve an item of his clothing.

The reporter had been as good as his word and published a story that cleared Kiyoshi of any suspicion as a murderer but had sown the seeds of another erroneous belief that Kiyoshi was in some way gifted with supernatural abilities. The reporter had embellished Kiyoshi's dream story so out of proportion that to the reader of the newspaper it would seem that it was apparent that if

The consequences

Kiyoshi chose to do so he could contact the other side by merely falling asleep.

"At least the majority of the population would now believe that I am not a murderer," he thought. The problem of such an accusation is that even when incorrect after a period of time and the facts of the case become a distant memory; when people recall the event they come up with the word "murderer" and the name of the person or persons associated. A little bit of mud sticks as they say.

Kiyoshi dismissed the thought and comforted himself that in his case it would not be so. He reached for his coat and shoved the cat off. The animal jumped down to remain where it landed, motionless except for a flick of the tail to express the displeasure of such a rude disturbance. Kiyoshi pulled on his coat, wrapped his scarf around his neck and reached for his umbrella. As his hand grasped the handle he was reminded of his first encounter with Bartholomew. His mind held on to the image of the ancient seaman to stir within him a pang of guilt. He shook his head to dislodge the unwanted vision and hastened out into the cold day.

A gust of icy wind brought his attention to the task in hand: to visit the headmaster and present his case for reinstatement. He lowered his head against the north wind and set off to school.

The visit proved unsuccessful. The headmaster was not impressed by the newspapers retraction of its former editorial. The school had no room for notoriety or staff that attracted unfavourable publicity even if it was inaccurate. He also considered Kiyoshi's alleged supernatural tendencies to be slightly unwelcome in regard to the minds of his pupils.

Kiyoshi walked from the school; his gait that of a dejected man. The future at this point in time seemed dim.

Without a job he couldn't hope to win the hand of Kaoru nor for that matter pursue any avenue of pleasure. To find other work would be difficult, especially at this time when the economy experienced a distinct downturn and several of his companions at the local "watering hole" had been made redundant. Plus, the inevitable burden of the enormous bill from the constabulary.

Kiyoshi and the Grumpy Ghost

He stopped by the stream close to the supermarket and gazed into the water. As he contemplated his next course of action and how to break the news to his mother, a pair of ducks splash landed, feet out stretched into the stream. They shook themselves waggled their tails and paddled furiously against the current. When they ceased to propel themselves and took time to examine something of interest, the water soon carried them back to the point where they first landed. Kiyoshi watched them repeat the process several times before they succumbed to the flow and were carried effortlessly beneath the bridge and out of his sight. He could have crossed the road and seen them from the other side, but his mind whilst still on the ducks contemplated the deeper philosophical interpretation of their actions and the struggle of life against the odds when it was much easier to go with the mainstream.

He likened himself to the ducks in his struggle against the pressures and traumas of life. He had almost convinced himself that this was the course of action if one was to experience an untroubled existence when it struck him that the ducks, whilst a lot more comfortable, were not where they wanted to be, in fact they had gone in a totally different direction from their initial intention. Kiyoshi was hardly where he wanted to be in life and concluded that he hadn't struggled at all but behaved like the ducks, gave up, carried along by the wishes of others and the line of least resistance.

A swirl of powdery flakes danced around his head as he examined his recent philosophical observations. He had for the most part of his existence succumbed to conformity. He turned to leave but stopped when he noticed a figure approach the bridge close by.

He waited.

Through the whirl of snowflakes, he made out the features of a young woman. His heart skipped a beat. It was her.

The personification of loveliness herself, head inclined forward she moved slowly in his direction.

'Hello,' he heard himself say.

The consequences

Kaoru looked up, her face dotted with snowflakes.

He wanted to lick them off, to cover her beauty with amorous passionate kisses.

'Oh,' she exclaimed. 'Hello.'

"What did she know, had she read about his confession? Had she had time to read the retraction?"

Desperate times call for desperate measures and Kiyoshi was desperate. His fortune such that his devastation would be complete if all hope of Kaoru was lost. He had nothing to lose.

'May I walk with you for a short while?' he asked hardly daring to hope her response would be positive.

'I'm not going far,' Kaoru answered.

'I er don't mind, a short way is fine I would just like to speak with you for a moment or two.'

'Well it isn't really the best of weather to be talking outside.'

'Perhaps you're right,' Kiyoshi answered, and sensed that his opportunity was slipping away.

"Desperate times," he thought.

'Er perhaps if you have a few moments. I would like to talk to you about an article in the newspaper. Could I ask you to join me in a cup of coffee across the road?'

Kiyoshi nodded in the vague direction of a coffee shop situated not far from the supermarket.

'I really would take up very little of your time.'

Kaoru, through half closed eyes to protect them from the intrusion of snowflakes, glanced in the direction of Kiyoshi's gesture. The look of anguish on his face stirred in her a twinge of compassion. She had been aware of Kiyoshi for many years and sensed that he liked her. She'd spoken to him on a few occasions but merely small talk. He was Japanese, she was Korean, neither family would be impressed by such a union, his mother especially would not smile on such a relationship.

Kiyoshi and the Grumpy Ghost

Like most people Kaoru had a natural curiosity and besides, the warmth of the coffee bar was a far more desirable place to be than on a bridge in the snow.

Kaoru inclined her head in agreement.

Kiyoshi felt he had received an enormous voltage of electricity through his body.

The mere consent of this divinity to have coffee with him was enough to drive such trivia as unemployment and scandal from his mind. He gestured to Kaoru to precede him; they made their way to the cafe.

The warmth of the interior restored their circulation to some semblance of normality and Kiyoshi ordered two coffees and some raisin toast.

Kaoru placed her hands on the table.

'It's very cold today,' she stated.

'Yes. It's the weather.'

Kaoru forced a smile in response to Kiyoshi's remark.

'What did you want to speak to me about so desperately?' she enquired.

'Have you read the newspaper recently?' he searched her eyes as he spoke, unable to believe he sat in a cafe with the one person he adored more than any other. Visions of toothpaste, excrement, and broken glass flashed across his mind.

'Yes,' Kaoru answered.

'And what did you think? Did you believe that I was capable of doing such a terrible thing?'

'Mr Hirota although we have spoken a few times in the past I know that you are a schoolteacher and that you live with your mother. I have very little idea of your character. You could be capable of anything.'

This was not the answer Kiyoshi anticipated.

The consequences

'And what did you think?' Kiyoshi continued.

As Kaoru changed the position of her hands on the table Kiyoshi noticed the long slim fingers and smooth skin; he visualised them as they explored the most sensitive parts of his anatomy; he crossed his legs involuntarily.

'Well?' Kiyoshi enquired.

'I read that you didn't murder anyone, as previously reported. I was surprised when I read the paper.'

'What, you were surprised that I didn't do it?' Kiyoshi responded.

'No of course not, when I first read about you being held in relation to a murder.'

'But you just said that you thought I was capable of anything,' Kiyoshi interrupted.

'I meant that I didn't know you well enough to make judgements, but from the little knowledge I had of your character I was doubtful that you could be capable of murder.'

Kiyoshi bowed his head in acknowledgment of Kaoru's compliment.

'I am flattered that you took the time to read the paper, and come to such a conclusion.' Kiyoshi's heart pounded with each uttered word.

To be alone with her, to be in her company, for him was a great sense of achievement.

All thoughts of past events seemed unimportant.

'Tell me about your dream,' Kaoru enquired.

'What dream?'

'The dream, the one that kept returning.'

'Oh that one,' Kiyoshi answered and moved aside to allow the waiter to set down their coffees and raisin toast.

Kaoru leaned forward and waited for Kiyoshi to continue.

Kiyoshi and the Grumpy Ghost

The close proximity of such beauty distracted him from her words. Through the mist of his lovesick mind dawned the realisation that she expected a reply.

'Well er...' he stammered.

"To hell with it I'll tell her about Bartholomew, why not? Maybe she will be impressed by such a story."

Kaoru continued her observation in anticipation of a response.

'Do you believe in ghosts?' Kiyoshi asked.

'Ghosts? I don't think I do,' she said.

Kiyoshi searched her face for some indication that he should tell her of his encounter with the "other side".

Her eyebrows rose as she spoke.

'Why do you ask?'

Kiyoshi took a sip of his coffee, replaced the cup in the saucer and leaned closer to her.

'The skeleton that was exhumed from the park conveniences. The one I said I dreamt was there. It was a ghost who told me.'

Kaoru made no comment.

Kiyoshi continued.

'It was midnight a few days ago when I had this visitor; an English sea captain murdered by Dutch sailors who picked him up after they'd sunk his ship.'

Kiyoshi glanced at the plate in front of him.

'Oh please, eat some raisin toast before it gets cold.'

Kaoru wondered what raisin toast had to do with a ghost and realised Kiyoshi meant her to eat.

She looked at the toast, then back to Kiyoshi, her hand reached out and took a slice.

'Please continue,' she requested.

The consequences

Kiyoshi went on to tell her the story leading to Bartholomew's murder, including the conditions required to set his soul to rest according to the ghost's belief. He waited for her response.

'I never could understand the Christian faith,' he added.

Kiyoshi noticed Kaoru's eyebrows rise; he may have said the wrong thing. Or was it a reaction to his story?

He decided to cover himself just in case.

'Some of my closest friends are Christians I really must ask more about their religion in future. It sounds fascinating.'

There was a moments silence and Kiyoshi reached for the last piece of raisin toast as Kaoru digested what Kiyoshi had just told her. He nibbled the aromatic bread unenthusiastically and stared at the object of his passion as he waited for some sign from her as to what she thought of his story. She averted her eyes as the stare of her companion began to make her feel uncomfortable.

Kiyoshi realised and gave the raisin toast his full attention.

Finally, Kaoru responded, 'So you say that this ghost asked you for help. What happened?'

'Well I felt obligated to retrieve the man's remains from the place that they were buried and get rid of them in the ocean as he requested. You can imagine it was quite disconcerting to have a visitor from the grave ask for help. Unfortunately, the man's remains were buried under the ladies' toilet and the only way I could think of getting them was to get the police to do it for me'.

Kiyoshi failed to mention the fact that he had indirectly been instrumental in the demise of Mr Takashi, one of Kaoru's most ardent admirers.

'Well you know the rest; the bones were discovered and taken to Tokyo.'

'And what happened to the ghost?' Kaoru enquired.

Kiyoshi and the Grumpy Ghost

'Ah he went to Tokyo with the bones.' Kiyoshi felt a twinge of guilt as he spoke the words. But damn it why should he? He mentally cursed Bartholomew for making him feel this way.

Kaoru regarded Kiyoshi quizzically, then rose from the table.

'Thank you very much for the coffee. I really must be going.'

Kiyoshi's heart sank. She obviously thought, indicative by her manner that he was totally off his head.

'Don't you believe me?' Kiyoshi stated incredulously.

He felt panic sweep over him as Kaoru began to fumble in her handbag for some money.

'It's all right I'll get it.' Kiyoshi blurted. 'Look I'm telling the truth. Don't you believe me?'

Kaoru thanked him once again for the coffee bowed her head and departed.

Kiyoshi stared in disbelief at the few crumbs on the plate left from the raisin toast, all that remained a testament of their liaison.

"Why did she leave?" He couldn't understand it. He felt as though someone had taken hold of his intestines and twisted them. He rose from the table and made his way to the cashier's desk.

His mind went over the events that transpired in the coffee shop as he meandered home oblivious to weather conditions. His position seemed impossible. No job, no prospects of one his age, and most disastrous of all, his one true love lost forever. Plus, he had brought disgrace to his family; Japanese people have a tendency to believe that if a member of the family is guilty of some unsavoury crime then the whole family are tarred with the same brush and spurned accordingly.

Bartholomew had been a curse from the moment he'd forced himself upon him. Since his departure he had constantly been in Kiyoshi's thoughts like a bad taste in the mouth or the flavour of some indigestible food that repeats upon the consumer as a reminder of their over indulgence. He was struck by a thought.

The consequences

"If that presumptuous spook had been the cause of his problems he could also hold the key to their resolution."

He would go to Tokyo, contact him somehow and ask him to appear to Kaoru and restore her belief in his sanity. A glimmer of hope took seed in his despondent mind and his spirits took a turn for the better.

'I'm going to Tokyo,' he informed his mother

'Oh yes, when?' she replied in a half-hearted manner.

'First thing tomorrow morning.'

'Do you intend to confess to another murder?' She answered a note of sarcasm discernible in her voice.

Kiyoshi ignored it.

'I shall be gone for a couple of days.'

'Stay as long as you like,' his mother responded with a tone that suggested that she cared little if her son did not come back at all.

CHAPTER 6

The museum

Kiyoshi was up early the next morning, he had hardly slept, his mind preoccupied by the recent events and also whether he could make contact with Bartholomew. He decided to go directly to the museum and enquire as to the whereabouts of the skeleton. He assumed that Bartholomew would be in close proximity to his remains and the disgruntled spectre would recognise him. He was concerned it could be too late, and remembered what Bartholomew had said about a time limit on his existence in the same dimension.

The problem was which museum? Kiyoshi decided to call in at the police station and ask them where the bones had been taken. His arrival was greeted without enthusiasm; Nakayama was off-hand. Kiyoshi to a certain extent could understand the police officer's attitude although by the same token he had taken the only course of action he could under the circumstances. If the police had been amenable to belief in the spirit world and open to suggestion that there are things that do exist other than those scientifically proven, he would have told the truth. Although until Bartholomew's manifestation Kiyoshi would have been of the same opinion.

He gathered from Nakayama that Bartholomew had been taken to a museum in Ueno, Tokyo, where the bones where to be accurately dated and maybe at some later stage incorporated into an exhibit. Kiyoshi smiled to himself and visualised the response of Bartholomew when he finds out about the intention to display the remnants of his mortal coil to the general public.

Kiyoshi thanked Nakayama and set out on the drive to Tokyo. He decided to use the toll ways rather than go via the longer

The museum

coastal road. Although via the motorway cost more; now unemployed he had to consider his expenses.

"That's another thing I must do, go and see the welfare people," he thought.

"At least I can get some money for a few months while I try and find another job."

As he travelled his mind dwelt upon many things but mostly on Kaoru now that she seemed even more unattainable. He must convince Bartholomew to reveal himself to her.

It was two o' clock when he arrived in Ueno. The traffic from the outskirts of the city had been heavy. Another problem was parking, and after a lengthy search for a space, he was forced to drive away from his destination to find a spot. He then caught a train back to Ueno and made his way to the museum.

The weather in Tokyo was warmer and the trains perhaps too warm in contrast to the cold experienced when one left the carriage and braved the elements.

Although early in the afternoon the carriages were crowded and it was difficult to find a seat on certain lines especially those to Ueno, a very busy station which links up many areas and is one of the main destinations to pick up trains to the airport. Kiyoshi was not a city person although the atmosphere of Tokyo stimulated him with its throb of life and constant movement; the big department stores with their exotic and beautiful displays of goods and the bustle of the food halls; the lift girls in their uniforms as they stood in front of the vertical transport system and mouthed off their intended destination with robotic precision.

Expressionless they recited their well-rehearsed scripts.

The array of station ticket machines indicating the numerous subway companies and their destinations; the immaculately dressed station staff in their uniforms complete with hat and white gloves used to assist a passenger or two into the crowded confines of an already too full carriage.

Kiyoshi and the Grumpy Ghost

Kiyoshi looked up at the impressive architecture of the museum. He had been told that this particular building was where Bartholomew had been taken and decided the best course of action would be to introduce himself at the counter and request to see the bones. After all he was the one responsible for their discovery in the first place.

A crocodile of school children preceded him as he went up the steps and in through the entrance.

A woman from within a small box-like structure dispensed tickets.

"Another six hundred yen," Kiyoshi thought as he dug into his trouser pocket and pulled out some coins. He felt hungry and intended to get some food in one of the many noodle bars along the way but hadn't broken his journey and in no time found himself in front of the museum.

'I'll get something inside,' he half muttered aloud whilst he waited in the queue behind the school children. One by one they went through the turn-style. A little girl with a large shiny leather bag strapped to her back turned and looked at Kiyoshi. As she did she almost knocked one of her colleagues over with the encumbrance. Kiyoshi returned her gaze and was reminded that he should have been due back at school himself.

The crocodile of children moved forward towards the entrance.

At last Kiyoshi reached the desk. A bespectacled woman in her early thirties pushed a button and waited as an entry ticket oozed from a slit in the metal counter in front of her.

'Six hundred yen please,' she exclaimed politely. All through her previous ordeal of the passage of many excited infants clogging the entrance to the exhibits she had maintained an air of civility Kiyoshi was forced to admire.

'Excuse me, would there be any possibility of me seeing the manager or one of the staff in charge of the museum?' Kiyoshi enquired and tried to emulate the woman's manner without much luck as he was forced to raise his voice above the excited children in order to be heard.

The museum

The garrulous group were marshalled together and marched off in pursuit of their guardian. Kiyoshi tried again this time with more success.

'Without wishing offence sir, may I ask the reason?' she replied.

'I would like to know the location of an exhibit or future exhibit that I was responsible for,' Kiyoshi responded and hoped he sounded important.

The woman regarded him for a second then picked up a telephone.

'May I have your name please sir?' she requested with the same polite charm.

'Hirota,' Kiyoshi responded.

A few more prospective visitors began to line up behind Kiyoshi and the babble of conversation made it difficult for him to hear the receptionist. She replaced the receiver.

'The museum curator will be down in a moment, if you would like to wait over there sir, she won't be long.'

Kiyoshi was surprised that it was a woman; somehow he had expected it to be some grey-haired old man. He was even more surprised when she arrived.

An attractive thirty-year-old with a warm smile greeted him, she bowed courteously. She wore a white coat with a name tag on her left lapel, and a short navy blue skirt. Kiyoshi forced himself not to look down at her legs as she approached. He returned her greeting with a slight inclination of his head and at the same time stole a quick glance.

'Good morning Mr Hirota, my name is Yasuko Ishida, I understand that you say you are responsible for one of our exhibits, may I ask which one?'

Kiyoshi smiled totally disarmed by the woman in front of him.

'Er yes that's right, well I presume that it's here. The skeleton, the sailor's skeleton that I found.'

Kiyoshi wondered just how much of the truth Yasuko actually knew. He regarded her face for any expression of surprise. There was none.

'The skeleton, yes most interesting I believe you found it buried in a park?'

'Yes,' Kiyoshi replied and failed to mention it was under a public convenience although assumed that Yasuko knew.

'He was a sailor, an English captain killed by Dutch seamen after their ship was wrecked off the coast, they were on their way back from, I think it was China,' Kiyoshi continued.

'Is there any chance that I could possibly see the skeleton just once more?'

Yasuko began to think that Kiyoshi was to say the least, odd.

'May I ask how you "know" all these facts?'

Kiyoshi realised that he had blundered and that the curator's attitude showed signs of patronisation. If she thought he was in any way peculiar, he would have little chance to see the skeleton unless it was exhibited to the public.

'Well of course I don't actually know for sure that this is the case. I mean these are purely assumptions on my part, I studied a little history of the region and there was a small amount of early trade with the Chinese at the time. So I assumed that because of their age and of course with a little help from my imagination I made up the story.'

Yasuko smiled and gestured that he should follow.

'Please come this way.'

Kiyoshi beamed back and thought to himself that to walk behind Yasuko was a pleasure in itself. They made their way through a door that read "Staff Only", wound their way along a labyrinth of corridors and down two flights of stairs before they came to a small room. Yasuko entered, followed closely by Kiyoshi.

The museum

The building was old and had been one of the few to survive the great fire in the early nineteen twenties that devastated the city and destroyed most of the old wooden buildings. Many houses and structures that demonstrated the ancient architectural character of Tokyo were lost. It was started by an earthquake and was responsible for the deaths of thousands of people.

Tokyo itself is situated directly over an area where the earth's plates meet and it is considered by most residents that another quake of similar size is not thought of as "if" but "when".

Inside the room were many shelves and in the centre was a table cluttered with boxes. In one of the boxes were the remains of the ancient mariner. Kiyoshi peered cautiously within.

'There you are Mr. Hirota, your English sea captain. As you can see we have assembled the bones in their correct anatomical order and will begin the next process of wiring them up. The bones have been treated with a preserving substance and will later be varnished. We have tried to restore as best we can the remnants of his clothing.'

'Are you going to put them on display?' Kiyoshi enquired. He had not seen the skeleton of Bartholomew although in truth he never had any great desire to do so.

'There is a possibility; we are looking at the ethical implications of such a display. Although because of the age of the skeleton it's highly likely that they will be exhibited in some form or another.'

Kiyoshi nodded with interested as the young woman spoke and calculated how he could obtain the remains of Bartholomew. It would sound totally ridiculous if he offered to buy them and came to the conclusion he was up against a wall of insurmountable bureaucracy. He also wondered where Bartholomew was and why he hadn't appeared.

Yasuko finished her informative speech and looked at Kiyoshi with an expression that indicated the interview was in its final stage and she had other things to attend to.

Kiyoshi and the Grumpy Ghost

Kiyoshi picked up on her body language and politely informed her that she had been most kind and felt sure she was a busy person and he would take no more of her valuable time.

She made her way toward the door, opened it and indicated Kiyoshi precede her. He graciously declined and gestured that she should go first. This seemingly gallant act was no more than a sleazy desire to once more look at the shapely legs of the museum curator. Yasuko declined his offer and said that she had to lock up and for him to please go ahead.

They walked back through the numerous corridors that led from the reception desk to the store room, Kiyoshi of the opinion that perhaps his venture had been in vain and that Bartholomew had no longer the ability to access the same dimension as him. "If this was the case, at least he had tried" he thought, which helped to ease his conscience.

Yasuko bade him farewell at the desk and bowed politely; Kiyoshi watched her shapely form until she turned a corner and disappeared from sight.

'Now what?' he muttered to himself. He hadn't been to a museum for a long time and thought as he was here, thanks to Yasuko, and on the side of the barrier that people forked out six hundred yen for the privilege, decided to take advantage of the situation and browse around. He made his way to the ancient history exhibits and found himself in front of a picture of a semi-naked woman arranging flowers. He spent a few moments to study the art work but his thoughts were elsewhere. His stomach also reminded him that he hadn't eaten and he should make his way up to the cafeteria on the second floor to feed his face. He was well pleased he'd saved the entrance fee which would go toward the cost of his meal.

He walked briskly from the gallery into the main corridor of the museum passed several mounted figures draped in traditional Samurai dress armed with weapons designed to hack, pierce or disembowel a foe; each with a similar objective. Kiyoshi shuddered at the thought of facing an adversary with such intent.

The museum

He remembered his futile attempt to strike Bartholomew from the rear with his umbrella and mused what he would have done if there had been a sword handy. Would he have wielded it with the same enthusiasm?

"Of course not," he told himself. An umbrella is hardly a sword and besides his intention was merely to render him unconscious. He mentally wrestled with himself as to the moral implications of his attempt to strike Bartholomew when his nostrils detected a familiar odour. That of old tapestry, the sort of smell that exudes from well used carpets if they have been stored for a period of time and are damp, the smell of musk. Perhaps it is the museum Kiyoshi thought, after all the entire place is filled with ancient tapestry and carpets.

He was drawn toward an exhibit close to the exit. A figure dressed in bamboo armour wielded a wicked sword. He peered into the glass case and beheld the face of the warrior, carved from modern synthetic material, gradually transform into the recognisable features of Bartholomew. He stepped back, the image drifted from the confines of the case into the corridor.

'So you came at last,' a voice boomed, sending a shiver through his body. Although now familiar with his ethereal colleague, it still gave him a sensation in his spine that caused just the tiniest contraction of his sphincter. Nothing like as in the past but if one had the misfortune to be instructed to conduct a scientific experiment on the effects of supernatural experiences on the human body, and if one was to observe that particular anal part of the anatomy at the time of the manifestation, then it would be clearly visible to the naked eye that the muscle in question contracted with enough force to crack a small peanut.

In one way he was disappointed that he'd found Bartholomew, but in another, which surprised him, he felt that he'd followed some predestined plan and the sooner he fulfilled its requirements, the sooner he would be free of the ancient mariner.

He glanced around the immediate vicinity. There was nobody within hearing distance.

Bartholomew looked genuinely happy to see Kiyoshi.

Kiyoshi and the Grumpy Ghost

'My dear fellow I am indeed pleased to see you. I only have a short time left before I fade from this dimension and have to return to the curse of immortality.'

Kiyoshi couldn't think of anything to say. 'How are you?' he blurted out. 'I come see if can help.'

'You must help; I beg of you good sir. You are my last chance, I have just three days.' Bartholomew stated.

Kiyoshi scratched his head.

'What can I do?'

'You must get my remains out of this establishment and then bury me at sea with a service.'

Kiyoshi thought it impossible. Firstly, he had to get the bones out of the museum. He knew they would not just hand them over. Also if he put in an official request or went through the legal channels it would take months, and be costly to boot, plus he knew the outcome would be negative. To bury the damned things at sea would also not be easy. He'd need a boat, again highly costly or nigh impossible; as was the spectres final request for a Christian service. He might as well have asked him to recite a soliloquy from Hamlet. He felt decidedly inadequate.

'Maybe you ask impossible thing for me.'

'Nonsense,' replied Bartholomew his brows knitted like two large caterpillars on his ghostly forehead.

'Anything is possible; meet me tonight at midnight outside of the main entrance of this wretched building.'

'Midnight?' Kiyoshi replied in a falsetto voice.

Bartholomew peered at Kiyoshi taken aback by his feminine exclamation of the time.

'Midnight,' he repeated and faded from sight.

Kiyoshi contemplated the consequences of a midnight liaison to coerce him into a venture that he didn't want. He took a deep breath and made his way to the cafeteria.

The museum

A sandwich neatly packaged in one of the vending machines caught his eye. He then purchased a can of hot oolong tea and sat at one of the tables in the immediate area. He inserted his index finger in the ring opener, pulled back the weak metal and took a swig.

"Why bloody midnight? That means I've got to wait around for hours. Why not half past eight or seven o'clock? What can I do with myself?"

Kiyoshi opened his wallet. Whatever he did it would cost him money. He also knew what he wanted to do, but was it wise? And besides it would definitely be costly.

"Perhaps a film? What's the time?" He looked at his watch. It was three minutes past three.

"Nine bloody hours, maybe a film, then perhaps a visit to you know who. See how I feel." He took a bite from his sandwich.

It was six o'clock when Kiyoshi left the cinema. He'd waited thirty minutes for the previous audience to vacate the theatre and then joined the mad scramble for a seat once the doors opened. In most theatres cinema management sell unnumbered tickets and seemingly as many as they please, it's common for patrons to buy a ticket and then have to stand up throughout the film. Another thing that irritated Kiyoshi was the rush into the cinema in a most un -Japanese way, deposit a bag or alternative means of reservation on a seat, and then bugger off and deny another person access. An act not repeated in other countries as the items left on the seat would be nicked in a very short space of time. Kiyoshi had been fortunate and apart from the initial scramble spent an enjoyable two and half hours seated in front of the screen.

After the film he found himself heading for Kabuki Cho, a seedy area of Tokyo located in Shinjuku. He told himself he would call in to the club, merely to pay his respects and see if there were any familiar faces. He convinced himself he had no motive other than curiosity to visit the "Club Regal."

He paid the receptionist and made his way down the stairs.

Kiyoshi and the Grumpy Ghost

The place had an ambience of faded opulence and if one took the time to study the fixtures and fittings then it would be obvious even to the least perceptive eye that the place had seen better days. As Kiyoshi descended, the density of cigarette smoke increased and he found himself in the middle of a thick pall of tobacco fumes that hung in the air or what little was left of it.

The place was full, the majority business men, who chatted earnestly with each other or fondled the breast of some coquettish hostess. The girl, with well-practiced skill would invariably remove the offensive tentacle without any discouragement to the nine-times-out-of-ten inebriated patron. It was not in her interest to deter him parting with more money to slake her "insatiable thirst".

Girls could bestow their "favours" on certain clients although it was optional. If they wanted to earn something extra on the side or on their back, it was their decision. It usually took several visits to cement this kind of relationship; the women were mostly Japanese but there were a few Chinese and Koreans as well as a couple of Caucasian; the latter always very popular with the wealthier patrons, who after a few drinks, found any woman with fair hair irresistible.

If a Palomino mare had trotted into the bar or an Afghan hound, no doubt it would have been bought a drink and salaciously fondled. Kiyoshi on the other hand had no such preference and was most certainly not attracted by the prospect of an equine consort under any circumstances. Once in his early youth whilst travelling to Tokyo by train he noticed a field where several pigs grazed, the buttocks of a particularly smooth skinned sow were not dissimilar in shape and colour to that of a female of his own species; it merely served as a reminder rather than ignition of a desire for a porcine relationship, other than that of consumer and consumed.

Kiyoshi fought his way through the smoke and made his way to one of the tables. A young Korean girl came over.

'Hi,' she said, 'mind if I join you?'

The museum

Before Kiyoshi had time to reply her well rounded behind had already lowered itself on to the seat next to him.

She flashed a smile.

'What's your name?' she enquired.

Kiyoshi knew this liaison would cost him money.

'Kiyoshi,' he replied. 'I'm actually looking for Miyuki.'

The girl pulled a face then her expression transformed into a broad grin that lit up the whole of her features.

Kiyoshi was impressed with the warmth of her smile and wondered if this was a spontaneous gesture or a well-rehearsed way to lower prospective clients' defences.

'She's left,' the girl retorted, her face still with traces of her previous radiance, 'but I'm here.'

A fact that Kiyoshi was acutely aware of, he gave a quick smile.

'Aren't you going to buy me a drink?'

A waitress appeared as if from nowhere, the girl peered questioningly at her would be benefactor.

Kiyoshi regarded the girl before him with her bright eyes and sensuous mouth. Her tongue eased out and moved from the left side to the right in one motion to caress her upper lip with such delicacy that it took an almighty effort of will from Kiyoshi to decline her offer and rise from the table.

'I'm sorry it's nothing personal but I really wanted to see Miyuki.'

'I can please you as well as Miyuki,' the girl responded and placed her hand on his thigh.

Kiyoshi watched the long fingers as they began to move in an upward motion towards his groin.

Kiyoshi and the Grumpy Ghost

'I...' the sound that came from Kiyoshi was a high pitched squeak. He cleared his throat and spoke again this time with a husky quality in the tone.

'I really should be going, I...' his voice trailed off into a mumble and his eyes glazed over.

It was twelve fifteen when he eventually stumbled bleary eyed from the club, his mind clouded by alcohol. He had lost all track of time and his credit card had taken an undue wallop from which it would be difficult to recover. He had to get to Ueno. The last train had already gone and he had no idea where he was in relation to the museum. There was only one solution, a taxi. Stumbling into the road he peered up the street and made his way toward the station where there appeared to be more activity.

He tottered on unsteady feet, the effect of numerous beers evident to any passerby; the majority accustomed to the sight of middle aged men staggering home after a skin full.

It was twenty minutes to one when Kiyoshi finally got a cab and was half asleep when the driver pulled up outside the museum. Wearily, with hands that defied mental instruction, he handed the driver five thousand yen and tumbled from the taxi to land in an untidy heap on the pavement. The driver reluctantly got out, walked over to the spread eagled shape of Kiyoshi and stuffed his change into his top pocket. Kiyoshi stared up at the man through red rimmed eyes and thanked him for a really enjoyable trip. The cab driver bowed politely, climbed back into his taxi and drove off.

The entrance to the museum was set back in a small park; with a supreme effort he raised his body and made his way on unsteady legs to the arranged meeting spot well insulated from the cold by the amount of drinks he'd consumed.

Whilst alcohol offered him some value against the elements, on the negative side he found he was urgently in need of a place to relieve himself. A tree in front of the museum seemed an ideal place for such an act.

The museum

He lurched up to the leafless sentinel and with a great sigh of relief fulfilled the call of nature. It was whilst he indulged in this most natural of functions that he felt the most unnatural of hands on his shoulder. The shock of the icy touch caused him to utter a high-pitched screech and misdirect the contents of his bladder onto his left shoe

'Where have you been?' demanded Bartholomew. His tone of voice indicated he was not the happiest of ghosts.

Kiyoshi fumbled with the zip of his trousers and peered down at his foot which was just going through the warm stage of the proceedings.

'You make me piss on foot,' Kiyoshi retorted.

Bartholomew was not the least bit interested in Kiyoshi's moistened footwear and repeated his question.

'You make me wait much time. What can I do? You want me to wait outside Museum. Get cold. Too long,' Kiyoshi blurted defensively. 'You little bit selfish ghost. No you bloody mother fucking selfish ghost,' Kiyoshi continued employing the vernacular of Masaguchi's son whom he had heard use in class.

The reaction of the chemicals and alcohol in his system for the moment altered his perception of the world and his place in it.

Bartholomew regarded him with a bemused expression.

'Hmmm, such language is highly offensive,' Bartholomew responded not entirely sure what it meant. 'You sir, have been partaking of drink,' he continued.

Kiyoshi peered back at the hirsute sailor and nodded.

'Well let's get on with it then,' Bartholomew said impatiently.

Kiyoshi reached into his pocket and pulled out latex gloves and a mask. It was of Chiba Mariko, a small girl commonly depicted in cartoon and comic form.

'What in God's name is that?'

'This so no person can see face; I get feeling may need it.'

Kiyoshi and the Grumpy Ghost

Bartholomew gave a sigh of resignation.

Kiyoshi's movements never particularly quick in his sober state had slowed down considerably. He squinted at the museum through the slits in the mask.

'What we going to do?' He enquired.

'We are going to go inside and retrieve my remains.'

Kiyoshi said nothing as his mind struggled to formulate a response. He knew that's what Bartholomew would say, the thought had crossed his mind on the journey to Tokyo and he realised if he became involved it would no doubt be in the capacity as an accomplice to something illegal.

Without a word he turned and walked towards the museum acutely aware of his recently urinated on foot, his sock now on its way to the cold and soggy stage.

They reached the main gate, a security light shone directly on the door.

'It's too bright. People can see,' Kiyoshi stated.

'How can we get in? Maybe too difficult maybe should give up.'

'Give up?' Bartholomew boomed. 'Give up? When we are so close! Where is your courage sir?'

Kiyoshi wished he hadn't said anything. Then through his clouded mind a thought occurred to him that dismissed any sense of guilt. His mouth gaped open and he turned to Bartholomew, no sound came forth.

'Speak man,' Bartholomew said, 'the image you present is that of a large fish.'

If Kiyoshi understood Bartholomew's remark he gave no indication but continued to vocalise his own thoughts.

'You talk of courage. You have no problem; no person can catch you. If police or security comes you O.K., you just disappear. Just me stand with noodle on face and get caught.'

The museum

'Why are you talking about noodles? Come leave this to me,' Bartholomew stated dismissively. He looked up at the light, then vanished.

Kiyoshi pulled a face, he was tempted to stick out his tongue but decided against it for no reason other than the recipient of his displeasure was no longer to be seen and his tongue would have moistened the inside of the mask and generated an odour that can occur from saliva as it dries, to endure a nose full was not worth it. The light went out and he was plunged into darkness.

From where he stood he could see illuminations from the station and a few shops still open. His gaze alighted on something that if he were to crack peanuts with his sphincter he could have easily handled a tough one. A police box, and what was even worse, a policeman stood framed in the doorway.

'Let us go,' Bartholomew instructed.

Kiyoshi lurched after the figure ahead of him toward the entrance of the museum.

'Hey!' he shouted. 'There is policeman watching.'

Bartholomew ignored Kiyoshi and stopped outside the door.

'Policeman,' Kiyoshi repeated. 'He looking this way.'

Bartholomew shot a glance in the direction of the police box. 'He cannot see us worry not.'

'Very dark. Why did light go out?' It then dawned on Kiyoshi that it was more than coincidence that extinguished the beam of light. 'You make light go away?' he stated, his speech slurred.

Bartholomew turned to his companion.

'All right we'll go in. Get my physical remnants and then come out as quickly as possible.'

Kiyoshi liked the last part of the sentence best. He gave a sigh of resignation.

'How we get in?' he reiterated. As if in answer the heavy wooden door swung open, Kiyoshi was bewildered. 'How you do that?'

Kiyoshi and the Grumpy Ghost

'Don't concern yourself,' Bartholomew replied. 'Please enter and let us proceed.'

Kiyoshi looked over his shoulder at the police box. The occupant was no longer framed in the doorway and Kiyoshi assumed that he had returned to the small interior. He hoped he had.

They entered the museum.

It wasn't total blackness. There was a light, not very bright, but of sufficient capacity to illuminate the place and enable him to see his whereabouts. He wondered if Bartholomew had night vision, he was about to enquire but decided against it.

"Can I remember where the damned bones are?" he thought. "Surely the great hairy ghost can find them. But why the hell didn't he find them in my home town? I suppose he did," he mused.

'Follow me,' Bartholomew boomed. The problem had been taken out of Kiyoshi's hands and he fell in behind the ethereal form through the labyrinth of passages.

Several corridors later they arrived at the room Kiyoshi had visited with the Curator. Bartholomew opened it with the same ease as the wooden door at the main entrance. Kiyoshi was impressed. He took two steps and was greeted by an alarm loud enough to wake the dead, went into panic mode and fled down the corridor toward the exit. He was close to his destination when he felt the restraint of a powerful hand on his collar. He was convinced it was the long arm of the law and relieved to hear the voice of Bartholomew.

Although the tirade of abuse was hardly complimentary the majority of it, in ancient mariner speak, went over his head. He did glean that his companion was not happy with his behaviour.

'Quickly man, get back and complete our task! Are you so lily-livered that you run like a fowl when there is fear in your heart?'

The museum

The mistakenly assumed reference to flowers and vital organs failed to register but the word fear and run carried the gist of Bartholomew's sentence as Kiyoshi adopted a more sober state.

'Bells not good,' Kiyoshi stammered. 'People come to see I go to prison I in big trouble.' Kiyoshi turned to run back but was prevented by the grip of the ghostly hand.

'Courage sir!' Bartholomew bellowed. 'We cannot retreat now; we are so close. Quickly, we must finish this.'

Kiyoshi responded and expressed himself in Japanese his voice high-pitched and charged with emotion, 'It's O.K. for you, you Gaijin bastard, you can just disappear if the bloody police come, I can't, I will get caught.'

Bartholomew ignored him. Kiyoshi was about to continue his tirade when he was physically elevated from the ground and travelled at a great rate of knots through the corridors and back to the room from which he had fled. He was then dumped unceremoniously in the doorway.

'Please I implore you sir. Take hold of your senses and gather my remains.' Kiyoshi was disorientated after his rapid journey through the museum. 'Where am I?' he enquired.

He realised his location. Once again he felt coerced by his spectral tormentor.

As he entered the room, alarm bells rang in his ears.

Within the museum was a security system monitored from the top floor by two guards who stared in disbelief at one of the screens.

What they had witnessed was a figure with a ridiculous mask, gesticulate as if agitated and then talk to himself, followed by a burst of phenomenal speed that whisked him out of sight and into the screen of another monitor a considerable distance away.

Their expressions denoted they shared the same opinion. They exchanged glances in disbelief then raced down the stairs.

Kiyoshi and the Grumpy Ghost

In the meantime, Kiyoshi had managed to locate Bartholomew's skeleton and tried to arrange it in some fashion to make it easier to transport. Wires attached to several smaller bones didn't make it easy. He noticed a bag on a nearby table, which in his heightened state of anxiety prompted him to investigate. He grabbed it roughly. The bag fell open; two vases wrapped in paper not designed to cushion violent movement tumbled earthward. The paper as expected offered no resistance to the hard floor and the sound of shattered porcelain, which had survived the wear and tear of countless centuries, met an untimely fate.

'Bloody hell,' Kiyoshi muttered or the equivalent in Japanese, as he realised what he'd done.

'Oh my God they were probably priceless.' He regarded the pile of paper and shattered china but was brought back to the reality of his own predicament by the voice of Bartholomew instructing him to hurry. He rushed back to the skeleton and proceeded to fill the newly acquired bag with the remains. After a bend and twist here and there, he managed to finally stuff the last bone in as he heard the sound of footsteps. He froze in terror.

'Oh no I'm caught! I'm caught!' he repeated, a note of despair in his voice.

Kiyoshi reverted to his native tongue; Bartholomew could tell by the tone of his voice he was about to panic.

'Leave this to me,' Bartholomew said.

In the room there was a display unit which contained a full suit of Japanese armour circa 1778. An impressive piece of equipment fashioned from iron, lacquer and silk by ancient craftsmen, worn for ceremonial purpose. A long sword hung one side and a shorter one on the other. The two guards rushed in and stopped in their tracks confronted by the sight of the ancient warrior's apparel rising from the stand and advancing towards them. They backed off in disbelief. With a deft movement the long sword leapt from the scabbard and appeared as if held aloft by an unseen hand.

The museum

The movement of the silver blade as it swayed in an unfriendly motion was too much for them; they turned on their heels and fled.

'Now, good sir, make your escape,' Bartholomew instructed.

Kiyoshi didn't need to be told twice. He gathered up the bag and made for the door. There was a rush of air as the armour hurtled through the entrance ahead of Kiyoshi in pursuit of the two guards already on the third floor and still running whilst Kiyoshi ran for the entrance of the museum. He stopped in his tracks. Through the open door came two policemen, guns in hand; they advanced toward him.

'Halt!' one of the policemen shouted and aimed his pistol at Kiyoshi; he did as he was bid. They approached the masked school teacher, their guns at the ready.

'Barsolomew!' Kiyoshi screamed; his violent exhalation of breath caused the paper mask to rise and fall on his face. The police taken aback by this sudden outburst ceased their advance and pointed their guns with a more intense expression of threat. Kiyoshi heard a sound from behind him. He waited expectantly for the appearance of Bartholomew. For no apparent reason he was struck by the thought that his sock was still wet but warm again. Why he thought about this at such a time he could offer no explanation other than in times of acute stress it sometimes acts as a safety valve to dwell on something other than the immediate problem which can of course under certain circumstances be fatal.

Kiyoshi stood with an expression beneath the ludicrous "little girl mask" of smugness.

A look worn by one who threatened by a bully has their pet gorilla turn up at the right moment. He was confident the sight of the armour that towered above them, and the razor sharp sword that swirled in a vicious arc, would undermine even the most determined policeman in pursuit of his duty.

He was right.

The nearest officer raised his gun and fired six rounds in rapid succession at the breastplate and sent shattered fragments of material in all directions. Bullets ripped through the less fortified parts of the armour and ricocheted around the confines of the entrance hall. Kiyoshi's ears rang assaulted by gun fire. The museum curator would not be impressed to find her most prized exhibit riddled with police bullets. The officers of the law dropped their guns and emulated the actions of the security guard to flee in panic through the exit. Kiyoshi followed them out. He halted in his tracks to stare up at the camera on the door.

'Barsolomew san,' he said. 'Video camera see all we do.'

'What do you mean video camera?' Bartholomew muttered as he landed next to Kiyoshi.

The two security guards had returned to the safety of the monitor and peered at the screen. The armour stood motionless.

'He must have remote control over it,' one suggested. The other nodded in agreement and felt embarrassed they had fled from the scene without further investigation to determine the locomotion of the armour.

'Let's have another look.' The guards, their courage restored, made a hasty exit in pursuit of Kiyoshi.

'Get outside and I'll see you there,' Bartholomew said; he glanced at the camera.

'Maybe a good idea to go out of the side entrance.' Bartholomew nodded in the direction of the fire doors. Kiyoshi agreed and exited with the bag of bones to emerge with the sound of voices to his left. He dropped to the ground and remained still. Footsteps, and muted conversation with a note of urgency in the subdued tones, indicated that there were a lot of people involved and he was their subject.

Kiyoshi was already muddy and the commando style method of locomotion he used to put distance between himself and the museum only added to his condition.

'I'll have to have them dry cleaned,' he mumbled as he crawled on his belly to get away. It was dark and offered him enough cover to put several yards between himself and the door before he stood up and walked toward the station.

It hadn't snowed in Tokyo but the clouds had gathered and it wouldn't be long before they emptied their contents. There were no trains but there were several people in the area that offered him some anonymity.

"I'll wait in the entrance of the station," he thought, adopted a casual manner and looked behind him to see if he was followed. The bones rattled inside the bag as the rhythm of his body moved them against his thigh.

No one in pursuit; he could hear shouting and the wail of a siren in the distance.

'Where's that bloody ghost?' Kiyoshi muttered aloud.

Although uncomfortable he decided to wait; he inspected his mud covered hands and knees. There was a drinking fountain close by; he made his way over to it and kept his eyes open for any sign of Bartholomew or irate museum staff. He placed the bones carefully down, pressed the button and inserted his free hand under the trickle of icy water. After he had removed most of the dirt he repeated the process with the other hand and shook them both vigorously to remove any droplets of water. A quick look at his knees and he could see, from what light came from the station, two dirty wet marks. The colder temperature reminded him that thanks to Bartholomew his sock was far from dry.

"Perhaps I'd better wait here," he thought, not wishing to draw attention to himself from the police box close to the station.

Bartholomew materialised beside him. The familiar musky smell accompanied his arrival.

'Where you been?' Kiyoshi enquired. 'Not good for me be here. Longer stay, more chance I be caught.'

There was, in spite of recent events, which had stimulated his return to sobriety, a considerable volume of alcohol in his system.

Bartholomew didn't answer but implied by a nod that there was need to leave as soon as possible.

Kiyoshi and the Grumpy Ghost

'I have to get taxi back to car,' Kiyoshi muttered.

'Hey you!' A voice from behind stated with rude authority that generally comes from observance of too many American television programmes.

Kiyoshi didn't bother to look in the direction of the impolite utterance, instead snatched up the bag of bones and took off.

He ran as fast as his legs could carry him motivated by fear and aided by a vast surge of adrenalin through his system.

The author of the voice was one of the security guards who began to shout to no-one in particular that he had located the felon. He hastily spoke into his radio and took up pursuit.

Kiyoshi continued his flight, raced past the station and down one of the many narrow back streets off the main road. Most of the buildings were commercial premises and he frantically looked for somewhere to hide. He could hear the footsteps of his pursuer and judged from the sound there was more than one.

He stopped in front of a small wooden house. It was a private residence but one used by a Tatami maker who had converted his front room into a workshop. Kiyoshi leapt over the fence and lay face down; he scarcely dared to breathe.

Unfortunately, the exertion of his recent sprint had stimulated his need for oxygen and his body heaved in an effort to supply the vital ingredient to his over-taxed cardiovascular system. Never being one to partake in any sport, his condition was not the best. As he lay struggling to maintain silence against his body's instinctive reaction to breathe, he felt something wet against the back of his neck. He turned convinced he had been discovered.

Instead of the long arm of the law he was greeted by a pair of dark eyes owned by a shaggy black face that was covered in hair. It was a dog, a very big dog, possibly with Newfoundland blood in its veins. Fortunately, it was friendly.

Too friendly for Kiyoshi's comfort; the prostrate position of the human seemed to convey an invitation; with a woof of delight it buried its nose in Kiyoshi's exposed ear and began to position

The museum

itself for some kind of sexual act. Kiyoshi could hardly shout, the last thing he needed was to attract attention. He had always liked dogs but in no way desired any kind of amorous relationship.

'Get off, get off,' Kiyoshi whispered, and tried to push the animal away.

Kiyoshi's whisper and his movement seemed to stimulate "Rover's" advances and he gripped Kiyoshi's lower half with his two front paws and began to hump. His oversized body resembled an industrial pump and shoved Kiyoshi around the small garden. Kiyoshi not only, to avoid detection, had to put up with the indignity of being entangled with an oversexed hound, but also to maintain silence and keep the animal's utterances and loud pants to a minimum whilst he wrestled with the monster.

The dog ceased, whether or not it had satiated its lust or become bored didn't really interest Kiyoshi, it had stopped. Unfortunately, its attention now focused on the contents of Kiyoshi's bag, discarded whilst he tried to preserve his virginity. The dog nuzzled them inquisitively.

To Kiyoshi's horror Bartholomew's tibia was extracted and was about to be carried into a corner of the garden and possibly buried. Kiyoshi reached out and grabbed the bone. The dog resisted and pulled in the opposite direction, as dogs do when they try to hang on to something they want, usually accompanied by throaty growls.

'No, no, naughty boy, give, give,' Kiyoshi whispered.

To whisper to a dog and expect it to obey a command, unless of course you are a dog whisperer is perhaps futile, especially when the dog is excited. The dog tugged even harder. Kiyoshi lay face down with his arms outstretched and hung on to the bone like grim death.

"If the skeleton wasn't complete, would it still give Bartholomew peace?" Kiyoshi thought as the strength of the dog began to prevail and he was dragged once more through the mud.

Kiyoshi and the Grumpy Ghost

Two policemen and a security guard came around the corner. They stopped and peered down the narrow street before they slowly walked towards the place where Kiyoshi conducted his canine capers. They heard growls and scuffles but could not pinpoint the exact location without going further down the narrow lane.

'He couldn't have got all the way to the end of the street in the time that we saw him turn the corner,' one of the policemen offered.

The other scratched his head and scanned his immediate surroundings.

'You look one side of the street and I'll take the other. And I'll check out that dog I can hear.'

The three men split up, two searched on the opposite side to where Kiyoshi lay.

'Where is that damned ghost when I need him?' Kiyoshi gasped as he continued to fight for control of Bartholomew's tibia.

The policeman approached the house where Kiyoshi wrestled with Rover. From where he stood, all he could see was the dog's tail as it wagged furiously. He was about to peer over the wall when a loud noise came from the other end of the street. It was a rubbish bin thrown with some force into the middle of the street, followed by another and then another. The men exchanged puzzled glances and then raced toward the cause of the disturbance.

'What on earth are you doing with that animal?' a familiar voice boomed. 'Get up man and for heaven's sake have some respect for my remains!'

'I am try to keep bone; dog won't let go,' Kiyoshi stated.

His tone indicated that he was annoyed that Bartholomew should think that he actually played with the dog, his head spun and he started to feel the effects of his previous heroic exertion.

'Please help!'

The museum

Bartholomew stood in front of the dog. The animal immediately let go of the bone, his head and tail dropped simultaneously and he slunk away into the corner of the yard.

Kiyoshi raised himself from the mud and examined his soiled clothes.

'Humph,' Kiyoshi muttered. 'Not good experience with dog, why you no come earlier? Maybe I meet you soon Barsolomew san in own level,' he exclaimed despondently.

He glanced over to the dog which sat quietly and watched.

'You naughty dog; nearly got me caught,' he scolded. The dog peered forlornly back at him with a doleful expression and sank to the ground.

Bartholomew didn't understand what Kiyoshi mumbled but nodded in agreement with whatever it was. 'Quickly! Before they return.'

Kiyoshi picked up the bones, stumbled over the fence and dropped the bag.

'Sir I would ask you to please, please take care of my mortal remains.'

'Sorry,' Kiyoshi meekly replied.

'Come let us make haste,' Bartholomew insisted.

Kiyoshi half ran, half staggered back around the corner then froze with fear. He could see in the distance another three uniformed men advance rapidly toward him.

'Shit,' Kiyoshi blurted and turned in the opposite direction. Again he ran, perhaps not quite as fast as before but at a considerable pace down the main street. He took the first side street available, then a left and then a right before he stopped for breath. He was fortunate to have a considerable start on his pursuers and raced down a slope into an underground car park. As he descended a police siren wailed and turned into the narrow lane, he was unsure whether or not he had been spotted.

Kiyoshi and the Grumpy Ghost

'This is all too much I'm going to have a heart attack I know it if this continues for much longer,' he gasped, his breath so laboured that it bordered on the convulsive. His head felt as if it were about to burst, there was one small consolation; his foot felt considerably warmer if not drier.

Bartholomew materialised.

'Why you keep disappear when I need help?' Kiyoshi enquired and increased his effort to restore equilibrium to his intake of air.

'I have been with you all the time,' Bartholomew replied.

'I think I seen by police coming down slope,' Kiyoshi panted. He pointed to some steps. 'We go up.'

'As you wish,' Bartholomew responded.

Kiyoshi walked slowly up the stairs to a reception area. It dawned on him where he was. From down below there was a flash of red and he knew that the police had driven into the car park.

Kiyoshi came upon a reception desk but nobody was there. They were in the ground floor area of a hotel.

'Why don't you take that ridiculous mask off? It's filthy dirty.'

Kiyoshi in his inebriated state had grown so used to it flapping around his face he had forgotten he still wore it.

He pulled it off and went over to a machine that dispensed keys to the rooms. Kiyoshi fumbled around in his pocket for some cash. He took out his wallet and pulled out his last five thousand yen. His mind grappled for a moment with the fact that he needed money for the taxi. He searched his pockets. Surely he didn't spend all his cash? His fingers still not returned to their full dexterity groped around in his jacket in an effort to locate any hidden notes and alighted on the pocket in which the taxi driver had stuffed Kiyoshi's change.

'Ah I knew I hadn't spent all my money,' he pulled out the crumpled notes.

'I'll need fifteen hundred yen for the taxi, five hundred yen for the toll, and the room is four thousand for two hours.'

The museum

Kiyoshi mumbled to himself as he calculated his expenses.

The slam of a car door and the heavy fall of Government issue footwear forced him to insert his money into the machine with as much haste as possible and grab the key as it was dispensed.

He stuffed it into his pocket and raced up the stairs. He thought of the lift but assumed if it was the police they could see the floor he exited, he couldn't afford to wait for the damn thing.

His room was on the fourth floor and his heart rate had dramatically risen with the exertion of the ascent of the stairs. He reached his destination; fumbled with the key, pushed open the door and collapsed on the large double bed in the centre of the room.

'Oh,' he groaned, 'this is too much.'

"Perhaps it would be easier if I just gave myself up," he thought. "All this adrenalin can't be good for me."

He lay on the bed and turned on to his back to be confronted by an image of himself reflected from a ceiling mirror. It was not a pretty sight. A middle-aged man red-faced and unfit, gasped for air covered in drying mud.

"I must do something about my health," he thought.

Up until now Kiyoshi had considered anyone who did any kind of exercise a pain in the buttocks. Their indulgence was usually accompanied by a smug almost fanatical adherence to some exercise programme which for some unknown reason the practitioner was under the false illusion that everybody else wanted to hear about.

The information related of their particular form of self-inflicted torture generally delivered to the bored listener with an air of superiority and judgemental tone; indicating they considered anyone who didn't share their views an inferior creature. Many exercise fanatics hold the belief that anyone with a gram of excess body fat is a complete slob.

"I must get fit, I really must get into better shape," he resolved.

Kiyoshi and the Grumpy Ghost

'What is this object for?' a voice to his left enquired.

A low buzzing sound emitted from an article held by a finger and thumb of Bartholomew's left hand. Kiyoshi turned in the direction of the sound. It was an article made from rubber that resembled the anatomical shape of the male reproductive organ. There was a click and the object began to rotate in a circular motion.

'This love hotel,' Kiyoshi stated. 'People come here to making love.'

'What has this device got to do with it?' Bartholomew added as he observed the gyrating phallus, with a curious expression. Kiyoshi knew that it was a curious expression; the facial features of Bartholomew were largely obscured by his beard but his forehead could be seen; it was wrinkled by a frown.

'Love toys,' Kiyoshi explained.

'Love toys?' Bartholomew repeated.

Kiyoshi leaned over to a small cabinet by the bedside and opened the top drawer.

He took out a battery operated device with a small plastic case attached by a wire that led to the battery. When switched on the case vibrated in response to the amount of current from the power source.

Bartholomew placed the rubber penis on the bed and took the small pink plastic item.

'I don't understand?' he said.

Kiyoshi looked at him. 'Are you married Barsolomew san?'

'I had a wife and three children.' Bartholomew flicked the switch that controlled the clitoral stimulator. The pink oblong object began to vibrate. Kiyoshi observed Bartholomew as he turned the instrument over and examined it more closely. The mushroom like head of the reverberating phallus on the bed still continued its circular dance like a blind mole emerging from the ground. The incongruity of it all struck Kiyoshi and he lay back on the bed and laughed out loud.

'What is so amusing sir?' Bartholomew demanded his tone of voice indicative of his feelings.

Kiyoshi continued to laugh.

'Not laughing at you Barsolomew san, just situation.'

'Well kindly refrain sir, I find it irritating.' Bartholomew dropped the object on to the bed next to the other "toy" and went into the bathroom where he discovered a large spa bath with ornate taps. The sound of water along with soft ambient music piped in from some main source, no doubt the lobby, burbled in the background in an attempt to create an atmosphere of amore. Various soaps and sweet scented aromatic oils decorated the hand basin; there was a large mirror on the opposite wall.

After a quick look around, Bartholomew returned to the bedroom to find Kiyoshi on the bed. Music "erupted" from the mattress as it moved, supposedly to enhance the act of copulation.

'Sir is this dalliance really necessary? Shouldn't we be leaving this place?' Bartholomew inquired.

Kiyoshi reached down and turned the bed off. He sat up and listened.

He shook his head to clear his mind. After a pause, he climbed off and made his way to the door, put his ear against it and listened.

'What are you doing?'

'I listening for police,' Kiyoshi responded.

'What on earth for?'

'To see if safe?' he continued a hint of indignation in his voice. The police had already departed having not seen Kiyoshi and were there on another matter altogether, which had been settled.

Kiyoshi and the Grumpy Ghost

Bartholomew shook his head wearily and promptly vanished. A moment or two he materialised in the same spot.

'They have gone,' he stated in a matter of fact tone as if he confirmed something that he already knew and insinuated by his tone that the recipient of the information was somewhat of a dork.

'Are you sure?' Kiyoshi enquired.

Kiyoshi could see the eyebrows of Bartholomew raise in disbelief that he doubted his word.

'I believe you,' Kiyoshi hastily added before Bartholomew had time to reply. 'I have quick wash.'

Ten minutes later Kiyoshi picked up the bag of bones and made for the door.

He stopped and if Bartholomew had been composed of a more solid composition he would have crashed into him.

'Tell me Barsolomew san. In museum when were in real hurry to escape security guard. You make me go very fast. Like when in home town I jump over truck. But when running from police why you no help?'

'Because is it possible for you to carry yourself? Can you lift your own body?' Bartholomew replied.

'No. But why this has to do with it?'

'Because you sir, were carrying my bones. If you were not, then I could help you. It rendered the act impossible.'

Kiyoshi understood that the bones made the difference. Why they made the difference he was none the wiser, to pursue the question further would only involve him in lengthy discourse and the chances were at the end of it he would be no nearer to understand anything in a clearer light.

'I see,' he nodded. 'We go now. You carry.' He offered Bartholomew the bag. Bartholomew was not amused.

'Just make joke,' Kiyoshi stated. He turned the handle, opened the door and peered down the corridor. A sound to his left caused

The museum

him to freeze in fear. A man and a woman came round the corner and almost bumped into him.

'Excuse me,' the man apologised and walked on.

Kiyoshi breathed a sigh of relief and continued down the passage.

Their exit from the hotel was otherwise uneventful and he was lucky enough to get a taxi virtually outside the entrance. He arrived back at his car at two thirty a.m. The effects of the alcohol less obvious but he had a distinct bad taste in his mouth.

He felt pleased with himself as he placed the key in the ignition and started the engine.

'Now, can I remember how to get out of this city?' he mumbled and scanned a road sign as he drove off. Perhaps if he had paid more attention to the road he would have noticed the big black American limousine that swerved violently to miss him as he pulled out. There was a screech of tyres and the car shuddered to a halt avoiding his left side by mere inches. Kiyoshi made an angry gesture to the other driver and stalled the engine. The door of the limousine swung open and out climbed a man who appeared to be assembled with all the physical components required to make up a human body except one item, namely a neck. The large man looked as if he had been stuffed into a tightly fitted suit and felt uncomfortable in such attire. He lumbered bearlike over to Kiyoshi's car.

An obscenity suitable for one of such appearance rolled off his tongue accompanied by an expression of such belligerence that Kiyoshi although familiar with Japanese profanity, as he was a schoolteacher, had to stop and work out what the man said. Instead of being intimidated, the remnants of the alcohol and the accomplishment of his mission to retrieve the bones of Bartholomew had given him a false sense of invulnerability. One that was short lived.

'Get lost.' He stated to the no-necked-one who towered, with bent ear and flattened nose all indicative of a violent past, above him. The aforementioned leaned down, wrenched the car door

Kiyoshi and the Grumpy Ghost

open, grabbed Kiyoshi by the scruff of the neck and lifted him out. He placed him on the bonnet of the car and drew back his fist in order to "punish" him for his insolence. The great fist with the sausage like fingers curled under the palm never completed its objective but was stopped in mid-flight as if it had come up against a steel wall. The hand was restrained and simultaneously twisted behind the no-necked-one's back and his solid form pushed forward onto the bonnet of Kiyoshi's car. Kiyoshi moved aside and stood next to his would be assailant.

He drew back his hand and cuffed the man on the ear.

'Let that be a lesson to you,' he said to the prostrate figure.

He seemed to enjoy the sensation of a smack to the ample flesh on the back of the man's head and was about to deliver another reminder of the brutes lack of manners when Bartholomew stopped him.

'Sir, I am restraining this oaf not for the purpose of your indulging yourself but in order that we may proceed with all haste.'

Kiyoshi nodded but couldn't resist just one last slap to the ear which seemed to Kiyoshi to beg of such attention. The man gave a yelp more of indignation than pain as Bartholomew simultaneously released him. He sprang up and regarded Kiyoshi with disbelief. He stood and stared, bowed low, turned on his heel and returned to his car. The door closed and the large black vehicle swished off into the night.

'Hmmm... That'll teach him,' Kiyoshi stated convinced he had something to do with the man's restraint and subsequent humiliation. Bartholomew said nothing.

CHAPTER 7

Reconciliation

It was six o'clock in the morning when Kiyoshi drew up outside his house. He was tired and grateful to have arrived back in one piece and had formulated a plan on the way back as to what he should do when he returned. He would bury the bones in his front garden and then try and arrange some kind of nautical transport in which to dispose of the skeleton. The part that had troubled him most was the Christian service.

"How could he overcome that problem?" He would give it thought after some sleep, but before that he had one task to perform.

He left the car, went to the small shed and retrieved a large shovel; returned to the garden and started to dig. It was still dark. The ground was covered by a thin layer of snow and extremely hard. He worked as quickly as he could; his body and mind cried out for sleep as in a semi-dreamlike state he continued to labour.

Another person also in a dreamlike state was his mother who, awakened by the sound of Kiyoshi's car had got up to investigate and watched her son's efforts to dig up the front garden. She was about to ask what in hell's name he was up to gardening at this hour of the morning when she was startled by his next action. He seemed to talk to someone but there was nobody there. He reached down into a bag and withdrew an object that from where she was appeared to be a human skull. She gasped in disbelief as he tipped the contents of the bag into the shallow grave and covered them with soil. They were, from what she could make out, bones, and if they complemented the skull that she had seen her son handle then they were human bones.

Kiyoshi and the Grumpy Ghost

She remained at the window to watch in silence as her son completed his grisly chore, then enter the house. She hastily got back into bed and listened. He bade goodnight to Bartholomew and threw himself fully-clothed, exhausted, onto his bed. In a few moments he was asleep.

It was nine o'clock when his mother entered his bedroom drew back the curtains and informed him that he had visitors.

'Huh?' he enquired through red-rimmed eyes as she hovered above him. He felt grim. He was convinced his head was in the grip of some steel vice and his mouth felt like the bottom of a bird cage or to quote another simile, the inside of a Sumo wrestlers Mawashi.

'Who is it?' he enquired.

'The police,' his mother retorted without expression.

The word police stimulated Kiyoshi's mind like an instant dose of some illicit drug and he sat bolt upright in bed but without the "high" that usually goes with such an act, quite the opposite, a most definite low.

'What do they want? Why are they here?' Kiyoshi asked mostly of himself as he tried to assemble his thoughts into a more coherent shape.

'I really wouldn't know,' his mother replied with her usual laconic tone. 'I don't suppose it could be anything to do with the bones that you buried in the garden this morning.'

Kiyoshi's stomach turned.

'For God's sake don't say a word about that I implore you mother. Not a word I'll explain later, please not a word.'

Kiyoshi's mother regarded her son with a look that said, what I have I done to deserve such a son? Then turned and left the room; he heard her voice as she descended the stairs telling him to hurry as the police were anxious to speak to him.

He got up and realised he still wore the same clothes from the previous evening. The mud patches on his trousers and jacket

Reconciliation

were dry, but still visible. He went to his wardrobe, took out his pyjamas and dressing gown, then hastily changed.

Nakayama and Mifune were seated next to the small table and drank green tea when Kiyoshi came down the stairs.

'Er... good morning,' he stammered desperate to appear as casual as possible. 'Sorry to have kept you waiting.'

'Late night was it?' Nakayama enquired.

'No, I thought I'd have a lay in. How can I help you?'

'Where were you last night Mr Hirota?'

Kiyoshi feigned surprise at such a question.

'I was here,' Kiyoshi lied.

'Can you verify this Mrs Hirota?' Nakayama asked directly of the sturdy woman. If there was any intent to intimidate her it was totally wasted on the character of Mrs Hirota who was as tough as nails and beyond response to such an act. She on the other hand was a woman of impeccable moral stature and one thing she violently opposed was lies, embellishment of the truth perhaps on occasion but to tell a blatant outright lie was a different matter. She had been this way all her life and had tried to impose her code of morals on her son with little success. She was not about to change her ways at this stage of her life.

'I cannot verify that I am afraid.'

Kiyoshi looked at his mother with an expression of horror.

'I went and visited a friend of mine last night and when I got home I assumed my son was in and went to bed. When I went into his room this morning at seven o'clock he was asleep.'

'So there is the possibility that he could have still been out when you got home?'

'Have you been out this morning Mr Hirota?'

'No,' Kiyoshi replied and avoided his mother's gaze.

Kiyoshi and the Grumpy Ghost

'I notice your car, I presume that car is yours the red one, must have been there all night then. When you came home Mrs Hirota, did you notice it?'

'No I didn't,' she replied. 'But when I got home it was very dark.'

'Where did you go might I ask?' Nakayama said.

'I went to my friend Mrs Ishida she lives four houses down towards the supermarket. Please ask her if you don't believe me.'

'That won't be necessary.' Nakayama replied.

'May I ask what this is all about?' Kiyoshi said.

Nakayama looked directly at Kiyoshi's as he spoke.

'The museum where the remains that we found were kept was broken into last night and the skeleton stolen.'

'Good heavens,' Kiyoshi responded with such an air of innocence that it took all Mrs Hirota's control to stop her from an expression that clearly indicated how she felt.

'Why would anyone want to steal such a thing?' Kiyoshi continued.

'We have no idea, we thought that perhaps you could throw some light on the matter.'

'Me? How would I know who stole it?' Kiyoshi replied, he felt unease creep over him.

'You expressed the desire at one time if I remember to keep the bones. You were quite insistent if my memory serves me correctly. You said something about it being very important that they were buried at sea. Am I right in this?' Nakayama stated; a smug look on his face.

'Well yes at the time I did ask that but then I realised that the authorities would know best. So I took no further interest.'

'Who looks after the garden?'

Reconciliation

'My mother is the gardener,' Kiyoshi replied.

'I sometimes help if there's any heavy digging or such.'

'I see, very nice Mrs Hirota, very neat. Although I did notice some freshly turned soil that seemed a little incongruous with the rest of the garden.'

'I am going to plant a tree, I er… just turned the earth over to see if the ground was suitable,' he responded, and realised he'd blundered. Nakayama knew about trees. Kiyoshi recalled the incident in the park and felt a cold shiver run down his spine.

'As a matter of fact you're just the man I should ask. Can you recommend a particular kind of tree that would be suitable?'

Nakayama beamed with pleasure.

'Of course,' he rose from table and made for the door. 'I'll just have a look at the soil and check to see how much room you have.'

'No please don't bother just tell me any type tree. It's not very pleasant outside. More tea perhaps?' Kiyoshi said desperately trying to think of something to say that would keep Nakayama from a poke about in the garden.

'No thank you. It's no trouble, come Mifune,' Nakayama barked and slipped into his boots parked next to Mifune's, exaggerating the disparity in size between the two items of footwear.

Mifune waited expectantly for Kiyoshi's offer of more tea to extend to him and was in the process to reach for his cup in order to facilitate a refill when Nakayama's command caused all thoughts of tea to vanish from his mind; he sprang up in response to his superior's request. Why on earth he should have to go out into the cold and discuss trees, he really didn't know but complied with Nakayama's desire and put his feet once more into his cold boots.

Kiyoshi and the Grumpy Ghost

Kiyoshi's heart sunk as the sergeant went into the front garden like some eager dog anxious to retrieve a bone before his fellow canines discovered it.

He reached the spot where the earth was turned and looked down.

'Let me see,' he remarked and kicked some loose soil with his oversized hoof.

'Do you have a shovel?' he requested.

Kiyoshi's heart sank even deeper.

'It's really not necessary to go to all this trouble,' Kiyoshi replied. He'd come into the garden in his dressing gown and pyjamas and although the weather was cold, felt distinctly hot.

Mifune had also reached the spot where the tree was supposedly to be planted. 'Why don't you put it over there?' he enquired pointing to a spot close to the house that looked ideal for a tree.

'That's a good idea,' Kiyoshi hastily added. 'Why don't we try the soil over there?'

He moved quickly to the spot indicated by the smaller policeman.

Nakayama was not to be side-tracked in his task to unearth the skeleton he was convinced was buried on the spot he was now about to dig. He shot a quick glance where Mifune had indicated, gave the smaller man a contemptuous look that went completely over his head.

'Are you cold sir?' the vertically handicapped officer enquired of his superior.

'Yes, why not come inside and I'll give you another cup of hot tea,' Kiyoshi interjected and emphasised the word hot.

'We can talk about the type of tree, I mean we've seen the soil, now you know what type it is. What do you think Sergeant, do you think I should get one of those fast growing ones, or maybe a bush of some kind?'

Reconciliation

'A shovel please,' Nakayama said in a cool unemotional voice which said by the tone and delivery a great deal more, and conveyed to Kiyoshi that the game was up and to stop his efforts to switch his attention elsewhere. Kiyoshi gave a deep sigh. His shoulders slumped forward and he shuffled off to the shed in a dejected manner. Should he confess and prevent this charade from going any further. He opened the door reached in for the shovel and turned to face the hirsute features of Bartholomew. He was momentarily startled but the circumstances and the events of the past few moments had drained any energetic response from him. He acknowledged the presence of his companion with a minimal change of expression.

'It's all over now. Me finished, in big trouble now.'

'What are you talking about good sir? You look as though you have been the receiver of terrible news,' Bartholomew commented.

'Exactry,' Kiyoshi responded.

'Pardon?' Nakayama said and reached for the shovel.

Kiyoshi handed it over and went back inside the house without a reply, Bartholomew followed.

'What's the matter?' he enquired his voice more agitated.

'They will find bones in maybe two minutes,' Kiyoshi added as he watched from the kitchen window.

Nakayama smirked as he raised the shovel and brought it down onto the soil. He placed his large foot on the shoulder of the blade and straightened his leg to use his considerable weight to its advantage and generate as much force as he could. The blade sank into the earth; he lifted the load of soil and eagerly explored its contents for any skeletal remains. There was none. He dug deeper and more enthusiastically as each shovel full of earth failed to reveal anything but soil and stones and the odd small piece of rock.

Kiyoshi was about to go upstairs to get suitably dressed for his journey to the police station when he realised that Nakayama's efforts were not as yet fruitful. From the window he could see the frustrated policeman become more agitated.

'Why not over there?' Mifune suggested and pointed to the spot that he had considered more suitable in the first place.

'Don't be such a bloody fool Mifune!' Nakayama barked and vented his frustration on his subordinate. Mifune pulled a face, totally at a loss as to why he should be the subject of Nakayama's ire.

'But good spot for tree,' he repeated.

Nakayama rammed the shovel into the earth and straightened up.

'Can't you understand the reason why I'm digging here has nothing to do with trees?'

Mifune stared blankly at the red face of Nakayama.

'The soil has recently been dug. A skeleton is missing from a Tokyo museum that the suspect found and wanted to retain where better to hide stolen property than to bury it?'

Mifune nodded.

'Hmmm rather a long shot don't you think sir?'

The senior policeman regarded his smaller companion with a look that would have melted cheese. He handed Mifune the shovel and ordered him to dig.

The policeman held out his hand took the shovel nearly as big as him and started to turn the soil. Nakayama watched.

'Dig more to the left,' he instructed.

Kiyoshi stood in shocked disbelief. He knew that he had only covered the remains of Bartholomew with a thin layer of soil. He turned to his companion.

'Barsolomew san, did you move bones?'

'What did you say?' his mother replied as she came into the kitchen.

Reconciliation

Kiyoshi found it hard to believe that his mother could not see such an enormous object as the great hairy gaijin inches away from her.

Kiyoshi was surprised to hear her response.

'Just speaking my thoughts aloud,' he replied.

'Really?' his mother answered. She began to sniff the air.

'Smells like something's gone off, and it's freezing in this kitchen, where's the cat?' she enquired and glanced around for the pampered feline.

'I have no idea, probably upstairs on the bed.'

'No of course I didn't move them. Why on earth would I enlist your help if I could simply transport them myself?' Bartholomew stated.

Kiyoshi nodded thoughtfully and went into the garden.

'Nothing,' Mifune commented, a bead of perspiration rolled down his cheek.

'You're not going to dig my garden for me are you? It's very good of you,' Kiyoshi interrupted, a discernible smug note in his voice.

'Do you think this soil is suitable then sergeant?'

Nakayama turned to Kiyoshi.

'Yes I think it would be quite suitable.'

'Did you come up with a suggestion for a particular kind of tree?' Kiyoshi continued.

'Maybe a weeping willow,' Nakayama replied.

'But I thought they had long roots and were not the best trees to grow near buildings.'

'Perhaps a cherry tree then,' Nakayama retorted.

'That's a good idea; yes, I'll give it some consideration,' Kiyoshi continued, still in smug mode.

Nakayama began to feel the hairs on the back of his neck bristle in response to Kiyoshi's veiled taunts.

'That's enough Mifune!' he snapped. 'Let's be on our way.'

Mifune climbed out of the hole and handed Kiyoshi the shovel.

'Thank you, you are most kind. Yes, a cherry tree is a good suggestion.'

Mifune nodded in agreement. Nakayama faced Kiyoshi.

'Our investigations have only just begun Mr Hirota. The Tokyo police are sending us down the video tapes later this morning to see if we recognise the person who broke into the museum. We'll be in touch.'

Kiyoshi's smugness vanished as his mind recalled the surveillance cameras in the museum.

"But I was masked," he thought. "There's no way they can identify me."

'Thank you I would like to know what's happening in regard to the theft of the skeleton that I found,' Kiyoshi said and adopted a nonchalant pose to appear as casual as possible.

As Kiyoshi waited for them to leave, Nakayama's hat as if caught by a strong gust of wind lifted off his head and hurtled into a nearby puddle of melted snow, remained on the surface for a second or two, and then sank to fill with muddy water and leave just the peak to protrude from beneath the surface.

Nakayama was dumbfounded, there was hardly a breath of wind. He turned and gaped in disbelief as he stared at his hat.

Mifune on the other hand wore an expression similar to Kiyoshi, that of suppressed mirth.

Nakayama puzzled the event for a moment and decided not to pursue the matter. "It must have been some freak gust of wind," he thought.

He was not pleased.

Reconciliation

'Fetch my hat!' he barked; Mifune was already on his way to where the soggy piece of headgear was located. He squatted down as he removed his gloves and with finger and thumb took hold of the peak to lift it at arm's length from the puddle.

There was an expression sometimes seen on the face of persons who seek to make as little contact with an undesirable object that necessitates handling. The action is often accompanied by the handler's head being turned in the opposite direction in order that the nose has as little to do with it as possible. It took a great deal of self-control on the part of Mifune to keep his head straight. The hat disgorged its contents and he waited until the last drip had fallen to the ground. Unfortunately, the last drip seemed to be endowed with some tenacity and clung on to the peak. Mifune gave the cap a vigorous shake, his fingers moist and the peak of the cap wet, he lost his grip and the hat propelled with some reasonable force from his grasp into a small pile of manure Mrs Hirota used for plant nourishment.

Kiyoshi remained straight faced and knew that any demonstration of amusement would irritate Nakayama even more. Mifune tiptoed over to the shit-covered hat as if he demonstrated some kind of reverence; he picked it up, but this time with nose pointed in the other direction, he handed it back to Nakayama.

The large police officer was livid; he snatched it from his vertically challenged subordinate and shook it vigorously. He, somewhat loathe to handle it, gave it back to Mifune.

'Here take this and get it cleaned,' he grunted and reinforced for Kiyoshi the apt name of "rhino".

'You will hear from me,' Nakayama stated and strode off, Mifune in tow with his arm outstretched in order to keep the faeces-lined hat as far away as possible from his person, between his finger and thumb.

Kiyoshi watched, still attired in his nightwear but oblivious to the cold. Perhaps the alcohol from the night before gave him some insulation.

Bartholomew appeared at his side.

'A pompous fellow by his manner.'

Kiyoshi didn't catch what Bartholomew said but nodded in agreement.

'Maybe he can recognise me from video,' Kiyoshi replied, and faced the now familiar features of his ghostly colleague as if he chatted to an old friend.

'That device which you pointed out to me is no longer functioning,' Bartholomew added.

'Huh?' Kiyoshi remarked.

'That object "Videa" or whatever you said, is not going to be of concern,' Bartholomew repeated.

'How come you know about such modern technology?' Kiyoshi questioned.

'If you are referring to my knowledge of objects that are driven by impulses similar to the workings of my own energy system then it is simply a matter of basic application. Like to use an analogy, jumping in the water and swimming downstream with the flow until you reach your destination.'

Kiyoshi puzzled Bartholomew's words not understanding half of them.

'How you get back swim against flow?'

'No need my good man, you just jump out.'

Kiyoshi again indicated that he understood but in reality had only grasped a percentage of what Bartholomew had meant. He was struck by a thought. If the bones were not where he left them earlier that morning, then where the hell were they?

There was only one other person who could have possibly removed them, his mother.

He hastily excused himself to Bartholomew, with whom he was on reasonably familiar terms, remembering his tweaked ear outside the supermarket.

Reconciliation

He raced inside to confront his mother then paused for a moment to think of the best way to approach the subject.

She was in the kitchen and had put away some tea cups when Kiyoshi strolled casually into the small room.

'Thanks for not saying anything.'

His mother ignored him and placed more cups and saucers in the sink. She turned the tap on.

'So you must have seen me this morning when I arrived home?' Kiyoshi said as matter of fact as possible.

His mother squeezed some washing up liquid from a half filled bottle and began to wash the dishes whilst she retained an expression of complete disinterest in what her son said.

'Look I didn't murder anyone.'

'I know, I read the paper. But now you steal,' his mother replied.

'Mother, I told you once before that a ghost visited me asking for my help. A large hairy English sailor, a gaijin; remember the musky smell recently and the change of temperature? And that bloated policeman's hat? Who do you think did that?'

'What hat?' His mother replied.

'Well if you didn't see it then it's not worth talking about. But my confessing to murder do you think I would do that without a reason? And why would I go to Tokyo to steal some bloody bones that I really don't want?'

'I have no idea. All your life you have done things secretly never telling me where you are going or what you are doing.

You have been to Tokyo before; and don't tell me you went to see an old friend; the whole town knows why you go up there, for a woman. You probably got drunk and then stole the bones for some reason, known only to the strange workings of your own mind.'

Kiyoshi and the Grumpy Ghost

'Alright, think what you want but I must ask you, what have you done with them?'

'I threw them away,' his mother stated in a cold matter of fact voice.

'Where did you throw them?' Kiyoshi asked and took a deep breath to maintain a state of calm.

'Where I throw most things I don't want? In the rubbish bin, the last thing I want is a skeleton in my flower patch!!'

Kiyoshi rushed over to the bin lifted the lid and peered in. It was empty.

'Oh my God!!' he shouted. They've collected the rubbish. What time did they come?'

Kiyoshi yelled across to his mother, a state of panic seized him.

'The same time as they always do on this day, eight o'clock.'

Kiyoshi had to think fast.

"Where do they go? Wait a minute, I remember, to the land reclamation area about ten miles from here." He was about to run to the car when he realised he was still in his pyjamas. 'Oh no,' he mumbled to himself, took a detour via the house, raced up the stairs, climbed into some clothes and ran down.

A few seconds later he turned back, he had forgotten his keys. His mother watched her son in bewilderment and continued to wash the cups. Kiyoshi rushed into the kitchen.

'Did you wrap them in anything or just throw them in as they were?'

'I put them in a rubbish bag,' his mother replied and shook some soap suds off one of the cups.

'What colour was the rubbish bag?' Kiyoshi enquired a note of urgency in his voice.

'Black. If you took the rubbish out more often you'd know the colour.' His mother rebuked.

Reconciliation

Kiyoshi stood in the kitchen, raised his head and shouted.

'Barsolomew. Please I beg of you show self to mother!'

His mother looked at her son and shook her head sadly.

'To think I gave birth to this lunatic,' she muttered to herself and wished she could wash her hands of her son as easily as she washed the cups.

'Why don't you show self when I need you?'

'Bugger!' he said and again recalled a word that the unpleasant son of the equally unpleasant newspaper reporter often used to express his irritation.

Kiyoshi had no idea what it meant but it seemed to fit the occasion.

The expletive still rang in his mother's ears as he turned and ran for the car.

He drove straight to the landfill zone; his heart sank at the sight that met his arrival. Hundreds of seagulls wheeled and screeched in the sky above the tip to descend into the heart of the foul mass and search for food.

Their virgin white plumage in stark contrast to the dirty grey and soiled colours of discarded cans and packets of who knows what, that littered the area.

"Oh God I'll never find a small black plastic bag amongst all this shit," Kiyoshi thought and gazed over the vast tracts of garbage.

'Barsolomew!' Kiyoshi shrieked. He waited expectantly for the spectre to appear. Nothing happened.

'Where are you why you no help me?' he said.

'Why you no appear when needed?'

As he sat in the car and watched the gulls wheel and squabble over the rubbish, a loud horn blasted from behind. He looked in the rear view mirror; the shape of a garbage truck waited impatiently for him to move. He pulled his car over, the truck lumbered past.

As the over-laden vehicle bumped and rolled on its way he looked up at the grim face of the driver behind the wheel. There was a faint hint of recognition. He slammed the car into gear and followed the smelly conveyance to the checkpoint. The truck slowed and then proceeded to pass the uniformed man on the gate. Kiyoshi was stopped. He lowered the window and spoke to the attendant.

'Excuse me I need to follow that truck, I put something in my rubbish bin this morning and I need to get it back. It's very important.'

'Which area do you live?' the man enquired.

'Hitawadai,' Kiyoshi responded.

'That truck has come from another prefecture nowhere near Hitawadai,' the attendant went on.

'Bugger.'

'Huh?' the attendant enquired.

'Nothing I was just thinking aloud. If I put something in my bin at say eight this morning, where is the likely destination of it now?'

The man thought for a moment.

'What's the time now? Just after ten. Well they would probably have dumped one load; hang about.'

The man disappeared into a small shed adjacent to the checkpoint to emerge a few seconds later.

'Yes, they came in just before I came on which was about nine minutes to nine. They're unloading over in the west zone this week, any recent dumps will be over there.'

'Can I look?' Kiyoshi enquired.

'By all means, you'd better leave your car and walk probably the best idea.'

Reconciliation

"No the best idea would be if I drove over there sat in my car whilst you rummaged around in all that filth until you found it," thought Kiyoshi, but he said, 'Thank you very much. You're most kind.'

He climbed out of his car to be greeted by an icy blast of cold air.

A foul stench of decaying matter and effluent assailed his nostrils; he wrapped his scarf around his mouth.

"Birds can't have any sense of smell," he thought. "Probably just as well in the case of seagulls when they choose a mate; their breath would reek of fish at the best of times."

Kiyoshi ignored the large quantities of fish that he himself consumed. Sometimes his breath, especially after a heavy night on the amber fluid, compared favourably with the aroma of the tip.

'Where is the west zone?' Kiyoshi inquired of the attendant about to disappear into the warm confines of the hut.

The man pointed in the direction of the truck that Kiyoshi had followed in. It seemed miles away. He thanked the attendant and walked towards the vehicle as it began to disgorge its cargo of waste.

"He probably sits down and eats his lunch there," Kiyoshi thought.

In Japanese society people who perform more menial tasks, such as rubbish removal or the upkeep of public facilities, are considered in some way inferior. Kiyoshi was at this moment guilty of such considerations. He trudged along the path taken by the truck his head bowed against the elements, his nose wrapped in his scarf.

'Where is that damned spook?' Kiyoshi mumbled to himself. 'I don't understand where he goes to.'

Many sounds assaulted Kiyoshi's ears, the rev of a heavy Mitsubishi truck, the clank of the tailgate and the grind of powerful metal jaws compacting the contents; the screech of gulls

Kiyoshi and the Grumpy Ghost

as they jockeyed for the best position to take first pick of the newly ejected rubbish.

"Oh my God! The compactor!"

Images of bones being crushed flashed through his mind.

Apart from the more difficult task of finding them, would it affect the situation in any way as far as Bartholomew's departure was concerned?"

Kiyoshi watched the truck pull away and bounce back onto the road. Exhaust fumes belched from the rear to add more obnoxious odours to the atmosphere. The four wheeled metal monster disappeared through the checkpoint on another mission to clean up the town.

Kiyoshi took in his surroundings.

He felt an urge to pass wind and gave in to the desire as he could think of no earthly reason to withhold.

"This is one place I can freely fart as much as I like and nobody would notice," he thought. "Probably be like a breath of fresh air."

Gulls squabbled over the remnants of an uneaten sushi and brought his attention back to the Herculean task he had undertaken.

"At least I can see the most recent deposits from the lack of snow."

He stepped into the west zone. If he could have smelled it and the air had not been tainted by the foul stench of the tip, his olfactory nerve would have conveyed to him the heavy odour of musk. He had just begun to prod about in a half-hearted manner when the voice of Bartholomew rang in his ear.

He was startled but made a quick recovery as he recognised the author of the sound.

'What are you doing here?' Bartholomew demanded.

'Oh, just felt like walk,' Kiyoshi replied sarcastically.

Reconciliation

Bartholomew raised one eyebrow.

'I come here because as you know your bones not where I put last night. I ask mother where they are and she says she put them in rubbish bin so I come here to try and find.'

'Save yourself the trouble. They are in the small building.'

'What small building?' Kiyoshi inquired.

'The one that houses the instruments for the garden,'

'The mean bitch.'

'Pardon?' Bartholomew stated.

'We must return post-haste and perform the last part of the ritual,' he continued.

Kiyoshi was not too sure about the "post-haste" bit but gathered that Bartholomew wanted to get on with the last part.

Kiyoshi looked toward his car. It was a long way off. The thought that he must trudge through the foul rubbish and ice cold wind, filled him with gloom.

'It long way back,' he muttered and headed for his car.

As he took the first step he felt himself take to the air engulfed in a blue light.

The ground rushed past him at a tremendous rate of knots, cigarette and serial packets and a multitude of other items came and vanished in the blink of an eye. By the time he had gathered his wits in order to vocalise his predicament he was deposited by the door of his vehicle.

Two men conversed a few feet from him.

'The bloody idiot now wants it back.'

They scoured the area where Kiyoshi had been seconds ago. One of them wore a supercilious expression; he peered in the direction where Kiyoshi was last sighted.

'Can't see him now,' he said, his eyes narrowed on the false assumption that such an act would enhance his vision. The recipient of the man's question noticed Kiyoshi and looked puzzled. He nudged his companion.

'What?' he inquired.

'Isn't that him?' he nodded in the direction of Kiyoshi about to enter the car.

'Sit in the back,' Bartholomew said as he materialised in the driver's seat. Kiyoshi was surprised at Bartholomew's request but did as he was bid.

The car engine fired into life as he seated himself in the rear of the car.

The men gaped and stared intently to see the person who sat behind the wheel. There was nobody; the men said nothing.

Kiyoshi gave a regal wave as the car drove off. One of the men raised his hand in a weak gesture but continued to stare with an expression that resembled a pig as it emptied its bladder.

'Why you do that? Maybe I should drive now, maybe difficult to explain to police if stopped,' Kiyoshi said.

'Thought I'd make an impression on those two spectators,' Bartholomew retorted with a twinkle in his eye.

The two "spectators" were impressed but neither said anything, instead watched in silence as the car drove away.

Kiyoshi resumed the driver's position behind the wheel.

'Maybe doing last bit very impossible for me,' Kiyoshi commented to the hairy spectre sat cramped in the seat next to him.

'I know no Christian book, Bible. Where can I find?'

'I realise sir this land is mostly inhabited by heathens who believe in nothing. But I am sure that even here it is possible to obtain a Bible,' Bartholomew answered.

Kiyoshi racked his brain. He understood the gist of Bartholomew's words.

Reconciliation

"Bookshop. No wait, Kaoru. But would she talk to me?"

'Barsolomew san,' Kiyoshi stated in a firm tone.

'For me to get Bible I think you have to show self to Kaoru.'

'Out of the question,' Bartholomew retorted.

Kiyoshi stamped on the brakes and Bartholomew appeared on the opposite side of the windscreen positioned on the end of the bonnet. He slowly turned and faced Kiyoshi through the windscreen, then reappeared in the passenger seat.

'Was that really necessary?' he enquired in a tone of voice that indicated his displeasure.

'Maybe you should wear seat belt,' Kiyoshi stated.

'I want to say that if you no appear to Kaoru then I can't help.'

'You mean if I don't appear to Kaoru then you won't help?'

Kiyoshi sensed that Bartholomew's question was tinged with a trace of impatience and he didn't want to anger the spook for who knows what the consequences of such an action could be. After all an entity that could propel no small mass through the air with considerable velocity could utilise that talent in order to inflict terrible retribution for something that he considered offensive.

Kiyoshi turned to his passenger.

'Barsolomew san I help you and because of this I have no job. That's O.K. maybe I can find another. Mother thinks I really mad this time, I accept that. She always think I little strange. I spend time and money to get to Tokyo and nearly get arrested by police. O.K., I didn't get arrested, but police now think I am crook. I confess to murder because of you. Many bad things I do. This still O.K. But one thing I really want is Kaoru and worst thing to happen is that she thinks I totally crazy. Please all I ask you show self to her. I know maybe perhaps battery running low and you can't show yourself too much, if she believe then maybe she help us.'

Bartholomew looked at the school teacher.

Kiyoshi and the Grumpy Ghost

'I am unfamiliar with the letters O. and K. but I deduce that they are some kind of substitute for the words "all" and "right" in the context that you use them. I don't think that appearing to your woman is exactly O.K.,' and with that Bartholomew vanished.

Kiyoshi waited.

'Very rude person,' he muttered, put his foot down on the accelerator and moved off.

He mulled over recent events as he drove.

"What was he to do for a job? Maybe he should move to Tokyo although things weren't too good as far as job prospects there."

Many thoughts raced through his mind.

Bartholomew failed to materialise. Kiyoshi pulled up outside his house and went to the small shed. There were a few garden implements and several sacks of compost stacked in one corner. A black plastic rubbish bag caught his eye. He pulled it out, opened it and peered in. The clearly identifiable yellow skull grinned back from eyeless sockets and the lower jaw gaped open. Kiyoshi closed it. Although it was several hundred years old it still stirred within him a desire to have as little to do with it as possible. He replaced the bones and covered them with one of the sacks.

His mother was in front of the rice cooker when Kiyoshi walked in. She hardly cast a glance in her son's direction but continued preparation of food for lunch. Kiyoshi watched her but said nothing, choosing to avoid the issue rather than confront it.

"I'll deal with that particular problem later," he thought. At that moment his mind was solely occupied with the issue of how to win the affection of Kaoru. Perhaps as he hadn't seen Bartholomew lately it indicated the spook had complied with his request and Kaoru understood his predicament and her opinion of his mental health had a more positive outlook.

"I'll call her." He made his way upstairs to his room and took out his mobile phone. He knew where she worked and searched

Reconciliation

the net for the necessary information. Kiyoshi tapped in the numbers, his hand trembled and his heart beat faster in anticipation to hear the one sound in the world that sent tremors of pleasure through him.

A voice answered, a voice that caused a power surge of blood to rush to his brain. He spoke.

'Kaoru san?' He knew full well it was her.

'Yes.'

'It's me Hirota Kiyoshi,' continuing before Kaoru could interrupt, 'I'm sorry to call you at work but I wanted to ask you if anything strange or unusual has happened this morning?'

There was a pause and then Kaoru answered.

'What?'

'Anything unusual?' Kiyoshi repeated and wished he hadn't asked the question.

'No the only unusual thing is that you have called me,' Kaoru responded.

'Look I know I said some strange things the other day, and I'm sorry if I upset you but, er look could I ask you a favour?' Kiyoshi stammered.

'It depends what it is,' Kaoru replied.

'Do you have such a thing as a bible, a Christian bible?'

There was another pause before Kaoru replied.

'Yes.'

'Would you consider it a liberty if I asked to borrow it?' Kiyoshi enquired.

'Borrow it?' Kaoru repeated.

'Yes, only for a short while, just for a day.'

Kiyoshi and the Grumpy Ghost

'Why do you want a bible?' she responded, a note of scepticism in her voice.

Kiyoshi thought quickly. He couldn't tell her the truth and it was obvious the great hairy spirit hadn't complied with his request.

"I'm going to screw this up again," he thought, panic began to take hold.

'Kaoru,' he stated in a tone of voice that indicated something serious was about to be imparted. 'I really need a bible. I promise I'll look after it.'

'Why don't you try the library, I'm sure they would have one and what about one of your Christian friends you mentioned.'

Kiyoshi tried to think of a suitable response to her question.

'Well I'm not exactly the most popular person at the moment and I feel a little embarrassed about going into public places and my friends are overseas.'

The answer seemed to satisfy Kaoru.

'When do you want it?' she asked.

Kiyoshi's heart took an extra beat as the message from his brain carried the news that somewhere somehow there still glimmered a hope of some kind of liaison with the girl of his dreams.

'Well as soon as possible,' Kiyoshi said and fought to contain his enthusiasm at the prospect that he would again meet her.

'I'm at work now and I can't get away for another two hours.'

'I'm sorry to be such a nuisance and I'll meet you anywhere you like,' Kiyoshi retorted and struggled to sound blasé about the whole thing.

'Alright, make it at two o'clock at the café we visited the other day.'

'I'll be there.' The sound from the receiver informed Kiyoshi that Kaoru was no longer in communication with him.

Reconciliation

His mother noticed Kiyoshi's expression as he came down the stairs somewhat like that of the cat's as it lowered its corpulent body into a prohibited warm spot.

'I'm just going out for a while.'

'Really,' she said, and for once didn't bother to enquire of her son's reason for his inane expression.

'Right,' Kiyoshi replied and suitably rearranged his face in order to prevent any more questions.

She stared at him and remembered happier times when he behaved like a respectful son.

'It's still quite cold out. I'd put something warm on if I were you.'

The comment was totally lost on her offspring who had disappeared into the front room to look for a clean shirt. He needed to appear his best to meet Kaoru in order to create the impression he wanted.

As the time drew near Kiyoshi became more paranoid about his appearance and continually returned to the mirror to arrange strands of rebellious hair over his shiny pate. If only he had more hair.

He would often look at other more hirsute members of his sex and think, "Lucky bastards they take it for granted, and seldom appreciate their genetic good fortune. They don't deserve it."

It was one fifteen; a loud knock at the front door announced a visitor. Kiyoshi had declined his mother's offer of lunch and was in his bedroom. He went down stairs to answer it.

It was Masaguchi the local reporter, the big-mouth partly responsible for Kiyoshi's current demise, and the man whose semen had created another source of aggravation for Kiyoshi, in the shape of his know-all child.

The reporter smiled unaware of any antagonism on the part of Kiyoshi.

Kiyoshi and the Grumpy Ghost

'Good afternoon,' he stated in an over-friendly manner. 'Is there any chance of a quick word?'

Kiyoshi instantly thought of two quite suitable to express how he felt but didn't utter them; words that involved sex and travel.

'Why yes, please come in,' he replied.

The reporter stepped over the threshold and slipped his shoes off to place his feet into a well-worn pair of slippers provided by Kiyoshi. His mother came out of the front room as she exercised her false teeth on a chewy piece of octopus.

'Good afternoon Hirota san,' Masaguchi said and inclined his head as he did so.

Kiyoshi's mother returned his gesture and continued to chew the stubborn piece of tentacle.

'It's still very cold out,' Masaguchi offered, and removed his gloves. 'I hope I haven't called at an inconvenient time.'

'Well I was just about to go out, I have to meet someone,' Kiyoshi remarked.

'It's O.K. I won't keep you long.'

'Would you like a cup of tea or something?' Mrs Hirota asked having finally won the battle between her teeth and the octopus leg.

Kiyoshi shot a sickly smile in the direction of his mother.

'Yes that would be nice, thank you.' The reporter replied.

Kiyoshi showed Masaguchi into the front room, he cast a quick look at the clock.

'How can I help you?' Kiyoshi asked.

'Mr Hirota I understand that I have probably caused you a lot of hardship recently. But you must understand that I was only doing my job.'

Kiyoshi didn't reply.

Reconciliation

'So in order to try and make some kind of amends, my editor asked me to approach you with a proposition,' Masaguchi continued.

'Go on,' Kiyoshi said, a glimmer of interest ignited his curiosity.

'We understand that the bones that you discovered have disappeared from the museum.'

'Yes, so I am led to believe.' Kiyoshi gave nothing away. 'If you've come here to ask questions about the skeleton then I'm sorry I can't help you.'

'No, it's not about that, though of course we are curious as to the whereabouts of the bones. No, what I came to ask was if you would consider working for us?'

'What?' Kiyoshi responded, surprised by Masaguchi's suggestion.

'Work for us,' the reporter reiterated.

Kiyoshi's mother returned to the room where her previous encounter with her lunch had taken place. She heard the last part of Masaguchi's sentence and her ears pricked up.

'In what capacity?' Kiyoshi responded. 'I don't know anything about journalism.'

'You don't really have to. You are an educated man with a high level of literary skills and also a highly developed psychic ability.'

Kiyoshi was taken aback.

'We, that is, our editor, would like you to take on the job of writer of horoscopes and psychic adviser.'

Kiyoshi was about to object to such a ridiculous proposition when his mother perceiving his intended response to be of a negative nature, chimed in, 'That would be fantastic.'

Kiyoshi and the Grumpy Ghost

Masaguchi swung around to face Mrs Hirota, an inane grin on his face to inform the latest participant in the conversation, of his pleasure to hear positive affirmation of his suggestion.

'What?' Kiyoshi replied almost incredulously.

'An excellent idea,' his mother chirped, 'an ideal opportunity to use your psychic skills.'

'How long has he had these skills?' Masaguchi enquired.

'Years,' his mother replied and thought under the circumstances a small exaggeration was permissible. Her face contorted and her head tilted to one side as if she tried to recall anyone from a long line of super natural events.

'Can you give me any examples?' Masaguchi begged.

'He has dreams.'

'Dreams?' Masaguchi repeated.

'Yes,' Mrs Hirota replied, her brow knitted in concentration.

'He often speaks to himself in a foreign tongue.'

Kiyoshi was perplexed at his mother's enthusiasm to bend the truth after years of reprimanding him for his efforts to do just that.

'Look I have to leave,' Kiyoshi interrupted.

Masaguchi didn't know which way to turn; whether to continue with questions to Mrs Hirota or get a response from Kiyoshi. He chose the latter.

'Well, would you consider it? You'd probably earn far more than you did as a school teacher.'

The last part of Masaguchi's sentence struck the right chord in Kiyoshi's mental apparatus.

Certain chemicals were secreted within the grey matter that prompted the recipient to assume a more receptive state of mind to suggestions. Unfortunately, they never reached saturation point as Kiyoshi was consumed with the desire to exit as hastily as possible.

Reconciliation

'You will really have to excuse me, you caught me at a bad time, I must apologise but I have to meet someone, it's very important.'

Kiyoshi's mother glared at her son but refrained from a rebuke in front of Masaguchi.

'Will you consider it?' Masaguchi enquired.

'I will,' Kiyoshi replied. 'I'll call in to your office first thing tomorrow morning and we can discuss it.'

Kiyoshi had already started to wrap his scarf around his neck as he spoke.

Masaguchi got the message.

'Right, er, I can see you are in a bit of a hurry, I'd better go then, I'll see you tomorrow.'

'Yes,' Kiyoshi said and almost shoved the reporter toward the door.

Masaguchi bowed low to Mrs Hirota.

'Don't you want your tea?' she enquired.

Kiyoshi looked at Masaguchi with an expression that indicated that this would not be a good idea.

'Er some other time perhaps, thanks all the same,' he replied.

Kiyoshi didn't want to leave his mother and Masaguchi alone together as no doubt by the time she'd finished with anecdotes of a supernatural kind, Masaguchi would be convinced that Kiyoshi was some kind of mystic Messiah.

He got rid of the reporter and left the house avoiding his mother's displeasure at his impolite manner.

He raced toward the café; it was five minutes to two; his heart pounded as he entered the warm interior. The proprietor greeted him with the customary acknowledgement to anybody who comes through the door. Kiyoshi didn't reply he glanced around the cafe and caught sight of Kaoru seated in a corner; she scanned the menu. Kiyoshi made his way across the room. Kaoru saw him

Kiyoshi and the Grumpy Ghost

approach. She inclined her head and greeted him; Kiyoshi returned the gesture, drew up a chair and sat opposite her. There was a bible on the table.

'Have you ordered?' he asked

'No not yet.'

Kiyoshi smiled politely and looked around the restaurant. He took off his coat and hung it over the back of the chair. Kaoru continued to study the menu then placed it in front of her. Kiyoshi leaned across, picked it up and excused himself as he did so.

'What are you going to have then?' he enquired and refrained to look in her direction. It was in an effort not stare for fear it may embarrass.

'Miso soup and Tempura,' Kaoru replied.

'Hmmm,' Kiyoshi studied the menu with renewed intent to force himself to concentrate on the mundane decision of what dish to choose whilst his mind was preoccupied with matters that provided more stimulation.

'So Hirota san why do you wish to borrow a bible?'

Kiyoshi lowered the menu.

'I er…' he mumbled desperately to think of a reason that would convince Kaoru to part with her book. His explanation was put on hold as the waiter appeared and asked for their orders.

'Well?' Kaoru repeated after the waiter left. Kiyoshi remained silent.

'I er…' Kiyoshi glanced around, there were two people seated at the table next to them but they were engrossed in their own conversation to listen to anything else.

'Remember the skeleton that I discovered?'

Kaoru nodded 'Yes.'

'Well it's, how can I explain, it's just that I er feel that the remains should have a Christian burial.'

Reconciliation

Kaoru looked at Kiyoshi in a way that told him she was not impressed.

'I read in the paper that the skeleton was stolen from the museum,' Kaoru added.

Kiyoshi looked over his shoulder.

'I know, I took it.'

Kaoru was even less impressed with this latest admission.

'And there was damage done to several exhibits,' she added with a note of disapproval.

'What I'm telling you sounds ludicrous I know and not exactly what you really want to hear, but I had to do it in order that the owner of the bones can find peace and I can find peace.'

Kaoru thought over what Kiyoshi had said.

'He only has a little time left before he is condemned to remain in another dimension.'

'Who is?' Kaoru asked tentatively.

'Barsolomew san.'

'Who is Barsolomew san?'

'The owner of the bones,' Kiyoshi stated.

'I'm sorry I don't understand.'

Kiyoshi looked into the face of the young woman opposite. Her brow wrinkled in an expression of puzzlement and disbelief. She was firmly convinced that Kiyoshi had snapped.

'Have you seen him at all?' Kiyoshi asked.

'Er... no, I don't think I have,' Kaoru replied and decided the best course of action would be to humour him.

'I asked him to appear to you but he obviously hasn't. I haven't seen him since we were at the tip.'

'The tip?' Kaoru repeated.

'Yes, I thought the bones had been taken away by the garbage collectors so I went to the tip to see if I could find them but they were in the shed all the time; God that place stinks.'

'The shed stinks?' Kaoru was puzzled.

'No the tip stinks.'

Kaoru nodded, 'Yes, I'm sure it does.'

'The bones, they were in the shed?'

'It's a long story, my mother put them there.'

'Your mother?' Kaoru asked, surely Mrs Hirota wasn't in any way involved with her son's insanity.

'So that's why I want a bible, so that I can say a few words over the remains and I was thinking that perhaps you would tell me the text they use at funerals. You are a Christian aren't you?'

Kaoru nodded.

'The only other problem is that the bones have to be buried in the sea, you don't have a boat do you?'

'No, not on me I'm afraid.'

The waiter arrived with their dishes and placed them down on the table.

Kaoru acknowledged the arrival of the food with the customary forward inclination of her head.

Kiyoshi leaned to one side to allow the waiter access to the table.

'Perhaps after lunch you would be good enough to show me the passage I need to use.'

Kaoru nodded, 'Yes, of course.'

She ate as quickly as she could and steered the conversation away from matters that would give Kiyoshi the opportunity to talk about skeletons and ancient mariners.

Reconciliation

After she finished, she hastily pointed out a service that is customarily used at funerals. Kiyoshi was grateful.

'I can't thank you enough; I will return the bible as soon as I have finished with it. The only problem I have now is to find someone with a boat.'

'I'm sure you'll find someone. Do you have to go to sea? Can't you just throw them from a cliff?'

'I wonder?' Kiyoshi mused.

'That's a thought, Misaki cliff, that overlooks the sea and is accessible by road, I can't see any reason why not, after all it's the sea and that's what he seemed most concerned about, I'll do it tonight. Thank you and thank you for believing me. You don't know how much it means to me,' Kiyoshi added.

They left the restaurant together and walked back to Kaoru's office where Kiyoshi asked if he could see her again.

Kaoru couldn't think of an immediate excuse and told him that she was very busy with work at the moment and would let him know.

In reality she had not the slightest intention to see him on a social basis again. She was convinced Kiyoshi needed help.

He, on the other hand felt completely dejected. He sensed it was a put-off and perhaps fooled himself all along that she could feel anything for him. With a sense of despair, he took a detour along the river back to the park where Bartholomew's skeleton was discovered.

He ignored the weather, wrapped in his thoughts, he tried to formulate in his mind the best course of action to take as far as his life was concerned; he sat down on a bench. Which brings us back to where we started.

After mentally reflecting on his past he became aware that he was not alone. He looked to his left and caught sight of the all too familiar shape of Bartholomew. He turned back and continued to stare at the ground.

Kiyoshi and the Grumpy Ghost

'Come sir, what makes you so melancholy?'

Kiyoshi ignored the ghostly mariner's remark.

'Are we not speaking?' Bartholomew continued.

Kiyoshi turned and faced his questioner.

'Why should I talk with you, I try to help and you no care about my life. I ask you favour and you go away. I can't get in touch. Why you no come when I want to talk? Why you no appear to Kaoru? I talk with Kaoru and she no believe me, I realise she think I mad. I don't care anymore. Do what you want, I no care.'

Kiyoshi blurted out his feelings leant forward and placed his face in his hands. He was about to continue with another tirade when he realised that his tormentor was no longer beside him.

Upon her arrival back at the office Kaoru returned to her desk and resumed work. Her thoughts of her encounter with Kiyoshi and what course of action she should take occupied her mind.

She came to the decision she must inform the authorities that it was Kiyoshi who stole the skeleton from the museum and responsible for the damage to the exhibits.

Mifune had filled in some paperwork when the telephone rang.

'Police, Constable Mifune speaking.'

Kaoru was hesitant but summoned up the motivation to inform the vertically challenged constable of what Kiyoshi had told her.

Mifune thanked her for the call, told her he would pass on the information to Nakayama when he returned and they would attend to it.

She didn't feel good about what she'd done and couldn't understand why she had pangs of guilt, after all she wasn't involved with Kiyoshi in any kind of relationship, and he had broken into a museum and stolen some property. He'd also been in the bizarre situation where he'd confessed to murder, not the sort of thing a sane rational person does.

Reconciliation

She decided to have a drink of water and went to the ladies to wash her hands. Her thoughts still of Kiyoshi; she turned the tap of the hand basin, glanced into the mirror and noticed a strand of hair out of place. She brushed it lightly from her face and reached into her bag for her comb; she turned from the mirror as she did so.

There were three other members of staff in the office when Kaoru's scream rang out, a man and two other women. All three burst through the door of the ladies to find the prostrate body of Kaoru on the tiled floor.

She was gently lifted and carried into the office where she was placed on a chair. As she regained consciousness she could just make out the blurred image of three anxious faces above her.

'Fetch some water,' the senior member of the trio requested; one face departed to reappear a moment later with a cup of water.

'What happened?'

'A man, a foreign man, very scruffy, in the toilet.'

The member of the anxious trio, whose testosterone level was considerably higher than his companions, stared at the door of the ladies' loo then strode purposefully toward it, pushed it open and entered. The door closed behind him. The three women waited. Kaoru had regained her senses when she was aware of an extra face looking down at her.

'Koshi,' Bartholomew exclaimed. 'He needs your help. I am Bartholomew,' the ghost continued.

Although Bartholomew had mispronounced his name, Kaoru had understood his meaning, her English perhaps better than Kiyoshi's.

She let out another scream that brought the concerned trio back.

Kaoru sat in a trance like state, her eyes wide open and filled with terror unable to speak; Bartholomew faded from view. The trio fussed around like mother hens as Kaoru tried to explain what she had seen. After much discussion it was decided that Kaoru should take the rest of the afternoon off. Perhaps she had eaten something which caused her to hallucinate, whatever it was she would be well advised to go home and rest.

Kaoru complied with her co-workers wishes and left the office, but instead of home she headed to Kiyoshi's house.

Kiyoshi's mother sat in the kitchen; there was a knock at the front door.

She was surprised to see Kaoru.

'Please excuse me Hirota san, is Kiyoshi san at home?' Kaoru asked.

'No, can I help you?'

Kiyoshi had mentioned that his mother had put the bones in the shed so she must be party to what Kiyoshi had done.

'It's about the skeleton,' Kaoru continued.

Mrs Hirota's expression almost changed.

'You'd better come in.'

Kaoru stepped into the house and removed her shoes; Mrs Hirota gave her some slippers and beckoned her to follow, they entered the front room.

'Would you like some tea?' she enquired.

'That would be nice, thank you.'

'Please excuse me,' Mrs Hirota said formally, inclined her head and left the room. Kaoru was about to pick up a newspaper when she heard a key turn in the front door followed by the sound of voices.

'Who?' She heard Kiyoshi ask.

'That Korean girl?' His mother responded none too enthusiastically.

Kiyoshi burst into the room.

'Kaoru, what are you doing here?'

Reconciliation

'I came to apologise,' she said and tilted her head humbly.

'What for?' Kiyoshi enquired and wanted nothing better than to lift her face and kiss her gently on the lips.

'I saw him.'

'You saw him?'

'The owner of the skeleton,' Kaoru continued.

'He appeared to me.'

Kiyoshi smiled.

'Thank you Barsolomew san,' he said to nowhere in particular but addressed the room in general.

'I came to warn you.'

'Of what?'

'I told the police. I am sorry.'

Kiyoshi felt a twinge of anxiety.

'What did you tell them?'

Kaoru dropped her head once again and looked down at the floor.

'That you said you stole the skeleton and you had it in the shed.'

Kiyoshi felt his stomach do a double turn.

'When did you tell them?'

'Maybe forty-five minutes ago,' Kaoru replied.

'Forty-five minutes. Why haven't they come here then?'

'I spoke to someone and they said that, I can't remember his name but he said he would do something or that he would tell him when he got back'

Kiyoshi pondered for a moment.

'We have to get the bones out of the shed.'

Kiyoshi and the Grumpy Ghost

He raced from the front room changed his shoes and ran out of the house to almost collide with his mother on her way into the room with a tray of tea and biscuits.

Kiyoshi located the bag of bones and wondered where he could hide them. He grabbed the shovel that Nakayama had used earlier, picked them up and made his way hastily to the spot where the portly police officer had recently dug.

Kaoru came out of the house and looked at the black bag that contained the remains of the English sailor.

'Is there anything I can do?' she enquired.

Kiyoshi stopped. He thought of many answers to her question, some of them not exactly what you would expect of a school teacher, but gave voice to only one.

'Perhaps you'd be kind enough to keep a look out for the police.'

Kiyoshi's mother appeared with a tray, two cups of green tea and some biscuits. It was not usual for refreshments to be served to guests in the front garden on a winter's day but protocol was ignored and she offered them to Kaoru who accepted with a bow.

To the casual spectator the scene would have conveyed a happy situation.

The man of the house dutifully toiled in the garden, his young wife at his side, and a thoughtful mother-in-law with refreshment for the happy couple. In reality the story visually depicted told a tale of a man about to intern a skeleton in his front garden watched by a conservative young woman who had just witnessed a supernatural phenomenon; his bewildered mother about to have a nervous breakdown.

Mrs Hirota said nothing. She had nothing to say. It was as if it were perfectly normal for her son to bury a bag that contained the bones of some deceased human in her front garden. If her son divested himself of his clothes and did some kind of primitive dance around the bag it would not have surprised her in the least.

Reconciliation

She looked at Kaoru and Kiyoshi, shook her head wearily and went back inside.

Kiyoshi replaced the shovel and walked back to the house when he heard the sound of a police siren.

He turned to Kaoru.

'Quickly you must go, I don't want you to be involved in this.'

Kaoru looked undecided.

'Please,' Kiyoshi insisted.

'Besides if they don't know that you are here then they will think I don't know that they know, or think that I know.'

Kaoru tried to work out exactly what Kiyoshi had said but gave up and deduced that Kiyoshi would prefer she was not around.

'I'll call you later,' he looked at her, through misty eyes.

'Will you help me?' he asked.

Kaoru nodded, 'Yes.'

Kiyoshi's reproductive organ twitched involuntarily and his heart skipped a beat.

The siren sounded louder.

'Please go,' Kiyoshi stated, a note of anxiety in his voice.

Kaoru complied, hurried down the path and took the opposite direction to the siren.

Kiyoshi had removed his shoes and changed into his slippers when there was a loud knock on the door.

Nakayama stood framed in the doorway; Kiyoshi assumed that Mifune was with him although he was concealed from view by his superior's bulk.

'Sergeant Nakayama,' Kiyoshi said and adopted an expression of surprise that would have done credit to the most experienced Thespian.

Kiyoshi and the Grumpy Ghost

'What can I do for you?' he enquired with an air of startled innocence.

'I have the authority to search your premises,' Nakayama cooed convinced that this time he had nailed the slippery little bastard.

'Search, what on earth for?' Kiyoshi replied.

'I think you know perfectly well sir,' Nakayama continued. Mifune's head appeared around the side of his superior officer's bulk.

'Constable Mifune,' Kiyoshi acknowledged, 'I didn't see you there'

Mifune gave a quick smile and bowed.

Nakayama had had enough of the formalities.

'Search the shed!' he barked to Mifune who was about to enquire as to Kiyoshi's state of health when his mouth that had recently assumed a shape to utter the first vowel sound, quickly changed into a stern grimace.

He walked over to the shed and went inside to carry out Nakayama's command.

Nakayama on the other hand oozed the kind of charm that smug people do when they feel that they have superior knowledge of some matter, and that knowledge is about to be revealed to the lesser mortal. Little did the large sergeant know that Kiyoshi experienced the same kind of sensation but without the unctuous facial expression. Nakayama and Kiyoshi both waited on the front door step the two of them faced the shed. Nakayama expected the re-appearance of his relatively miniscule inferior to emerge with the stolen bones; Kiyoshi to witness the humiliation of the tubby copper.

Nakayama's countenance changed from one who gloated to one who is puzzled. He strode manfully toward the shed.

'I can't find anything,' Mifune mumbled as the rhino-like sergeant thundered in.

Reconciliation

Nakayama hunted around the small interior and let out the odd grunt. It was obvious even to the untrained eye, there was nothing concealed in the area under scrutiny.

He strode back to Kiyoshi; Mifune followed and took several small steps to Nakayama's one.

'I'll need to search the house!' Nakayama barked, all traces of adopted courtesy vanished.

'Very well, if you insist,' Kiyoshi said and thought that whilst Nakayama was in the house then at least he was cold as far as discovery of the remains.

Although he appeared cool, calm and collected on the outside, Kiyoshi was anything but; banking on lightning not striking the same place twice.

Although the odds are probably even. Kiyoshi stepped aside to allow the police officer entry. Mifune followed.

After a fruitless search, Nakayama, visibly frustrated, managed to mumble a begrudged apology that had the sincerity of a politician's election promise.

He stood on the doorstep and looked out across the front garden directly at the newly turned soil. He replaced his cap and stared at the place of Bartholomew's recent internment. Kiyoshi could sense the man's thoughts. He felt a cold sweat break out. He had to act quickly.

'Shall I fetch the spade from the shed Sergeant?' he enquired with a hint of sarcasm. 'I could do with a bit more soil turned over.'

Nakayama faced Kiyoshi. He was in no mood for sarcasm.

'I know that you have something to do with the skeleton being stolen from Tokyo and I am convinced that you have the remains hidden somewhere around here. We shall be watching you very closely Mr Hirota. Please don't think that you can make fools of the police.'

Kiyoshi and the Grumpy Ghost

He took his cap off, perhaps remembering the last visit, stuffed it under his arm and snapped at Mifune; the two of them climbed into to their car and drove away.

Kiyoshi heaved a sigh of relief. He stared after the police car until it disappeared from sight.

'What did that girl want?' A voice enquired from behind him. Kiyoshi swung around to see the face of his mother at his left shoulder.

'She er... just came around to warn me,' Kiyoshi responded.

Mrs Hirota sighed her usual sigh.

'Is she married?' she asked.

Kiyoshi knew this was an opportunity that begged to be taken.

'Why do you ask that?'

'Oh no reason,' his mother answered.

Kiyoshi looked at her,

'Say I said to you that I would like to marry this girl.'

'Well are you?'

'What?' Kiyoshi asked.

'Saying that you would like to marry this girl?'

Kiyoshi paused before he answered.

'I don't know whether she would want to marry me. She's Korean.'

'I know,' his mother said.

'I think she wants to marry you.'

Kiyoshi regarded his mother once again but this time more intently.

'How do you know?' he asked, his expression one of acute anticipation of his mother's answer.

'I can tell these things.'

Reconciliation

'You wouldn't mind?' Kiyoshi asked.

'After all that's happened over the last few days, the disgrace you have brought to the family's name, I would be surprised if anyone would have you.'

'But you wouldn't object?' Kiyoshi continued.

'No, I've never said that I would.'

'But you've never liked Koreans, and I thought that you would automatically object if I told you that I wanted to marry a Korean girl. I will not lie to you, I would have liked it better if you had chosen a Japanese girl, but having said that I just wanted you to marry and if this girl would make you a good wife and give me some grandchildren, then I have no objection. The fact that she still speaks with you after you confessed to a murder and buried a skeleton in the garden, proves that she judges you in a way that is based on sound values, or that she has no values at all.'

Kiyoshi couldn't believe what he heard. His mother, a woman he'd known for over forty years, but never really known at all. He turned and faced her, for the first time in his life he saw her in a different light. She looked more frail than usual; he noticed that the elderly grey-haired lady in front of him possessed a vulnerability he'd not seen before. He felt ashamed. He was overcome with emotion. He remembered when he was a small boy if he cut himself or fell, his mother always afforded him love and support. He realised the roles had been reversed and he was now in the position to offer his support and love to the elderly lady before him.

He put out his hand and squeezed her arm, leaned forward and kissed her gently on the top of her head. It was not a gesture by Western standards to convey any significance, but to Kiyoshi's mother, who had experienced no physical demonstration of affection from her son after the age of eleven, it spoke volumes.

She felt a lump in her throat and tears, not of anger nor of frustration or sadness, but of reconciliation, trickle from her eyes. Kiyoshi took a tissue from the table and wiped the moisture from

Kiyoshi and the Grumpy Ghost

her cheek. He too felt emotions well up inside him and somewhat awkwardly at first, stretched out his arms and drew his mother into his embrace.

Nakayama fumed all the way back to the police station.

'I can feel it in my water, I know that pompous little fart is up to something.'

Mifune kept his eyes on the road and nodded his head in agreement at the appropriate time and said nothing, knowing from past experience that the best thing to do when Nakayama blustered was just to listen.

'I'll have him, Mifune keep an eye outside his house tonight I have a feeling that he's going to do something.'

Mifune wanted nothing less than to sit outside Kiyoshi's house on a cold winters evening and keep watch on the off chance that something may occur. He liked Kiyoshi and wanted to know more about his encounter with the "other side." He knew Masaguchi had asked Kiyoshi to work on the paper and had even thought about asking Kiyoshi's advice on the whereabouts of a relative he had lost contact with over the years, the police records came up with no solution as to his location.

'Yes sir,' he said and endeavoured to inject some enthusiasm into his voice.

'If anything occurs, call me immediately. Immediately do you understand?'

'Yes sir, immediately,' Mifune repeated. He hoped something did happen, if nothing else to deny his superior a good night's sleep. If he had to do it, it only seemed fair that his bulky boss should also suffer.

Kiyoshi was on the phone to Kaoru when Bartholomew appeared.

'All right six o'clock at your house.' Kiyoshi with a dreamy expression put his phone back into his pocket. His attention on other matters, he was startled by the appearance of Bartholomew.

Reconciliation

'Barsolomew san,' Kiyoshi bowed deferentially low.

'Thank you for appearing to Kaoru san for me, I am grateful.'

Bartholomew was unaccustomed to Kiyoshi's gratitude.

'It was the least I could do,' he stated.

'Barsolomew san. Time is running out; we must do tonight. One thing must ask. O.K. to throw bones over cliff?'

'Over cliff?' Bartholomew repeated in an incredulous tone.

'It still in sea, final resting place still in sea, and Kaoru san has said she will say words, but small problem, words in Japanese.'

'Japanese?' Bartholomew repeated.

'I don't know, I can see no reason why not, I'm sure the Lord can speak Japanese; thrown from a cliff, hmmm, I suppose a burial at sea is no different, the body is jettisoned from the ship.' Bartholomew turned to Kiyoshi.

'I must ask you sir one more favour. My remains, my bones, please wrap them in some form of cloth and bind them together.'

Kiyoshi looked quizzically at the spectre before him.

'Tie them.' Bartholomew demonstrated the action of wrapping and tying.

'So so,' Kiyoshi nodded, 'I understand.'

Mifune had sat outside Kiyoshi's house for some time when he noticed Kiyoshi come out. He was dressed in warm clothes and carried a torch; he made his way to the shed to emerge a few seconds later with a shovel. The police officer watched with interest as Kiyoshi went to where Bartholomew's remains were buried. A few seconds later Mrs Hirota came from the house, she carried some cloth and some chord.

Kiyoshi started to dig, Mifune reached for the police radio.

Kiyoshi and the Grumpy Ghost

The distance from his car to Kiyoshi was too far for him to see exactly what was going on. But he could see there were two figures engaged in some occupation in their front garden, hardly normal behaviour on a cold winter's night.

'They've just removed something, I can't quite make out what it is, I'm too far away; it looks like a bag or something.' Mifune whispered into the microphone.

'Why are you whispering?' Nakayama's voice bellowed back.

'If you are too far away it's unlikely that they can hear you.'

The irate voice of Nakayama continued as he strained his ears to catch his subordinate's information.

Kiyoshi withdrew the bones from the bag and laid them on the grass, his mother held the torch.

He'd told her the whole story from the start and although Bartholomew had refused to appear when Kiyoshi requested, she had chosen, with the added weight of Kaoru's tale, to believe her son. The other course of action would have been to dismiss him as a lunatic. She could see he was convinced of Bartholomew's existence and decided, having rediscovered their relationship, it was worth humouring him to preserve it. If to return to some normality meant to throw an old skeleton from a cliff, then so be it.

She laid the cloth on the icy ground; Kiyoshi emptied the bag and placed each bone carefully on the cloth.

'It's the skeleton.' Mifune stated and raised his voice.

'I'll be right there, don't do anything just stay with them.'

'I want to catch them red-handed,' Nakayama boomed.

Mifune continued his vigil.

After the bones were wrapped Kiyoshi tied and loaded them into the boot of his car. He bade farewell to his mother, bowed low and thanked her for her help. She watched her son drive away and felt things would be better from now on.

Reconciliation

Mifune waited until Kiyoshi had left before he followed.

Bartholomew appeared beside Kiyoshi.

'I can feel the moment is almost upon me. We have little time left.'

Kiyoshi put his foot harder down on the accelerator.

He cast a glance in the mirror but took no notice of the headlights behind him.

'Barsolomew san.'

'Hmmm?' Bartholomew replied.

'Maybe best if you not sit next to me when Kaoru get in.'

'I wish you would make up your mind good sir, one minute you wish me to appear to all and sundry the next to remain out of sight.'

'Maybe after Kaoru in car be better,' Kiyoshi said.

'You forget sir that I am only visible to you.'

'So Kaoru san cannot see.'

'Why should anything have changed? She can only see me if I desire it.'

Bartholomew stated a touch of impatience in his manner.

'I no wish to offend Barsolomew san but must admit maybe for girl you look bit scary.'

Bartholomew saw Kiyoshi's point and gave a smile undetected by his companion. The car drew up outside Kaoru's house and Kiyoshi gave the horn a tap. The faces of an elderly man and woman appeared at a front window. The door opened and Kaoru stepped out. Kiyoshi's heart raced at the sight of her. She looked even more beautiful than earlier in the day.

She ran to the car, threw a backward glance at the two faces in the window, opened the passenger door, climbed in and flashed a quick smile in Kiyoshi's direction. His elation due to her presence was only diminished by the thought that Bartholomew may appear at any moment and scare the life out of her. Perfume filled the interior of the vehicle and annihilated any musky odour that lingered from the recent departure of Bartholomew.

'Is that your father?' Kiyoshi asked.

'Yes, and my mother, they were curious although I didn't tell them anything.'

'I'm sure they were,' Kiyoshi replied, put the car into gear and drove off. He looked in the mirror and noticed car headlights behind him. Again, he failed to register that he was followed. The distraction of such close proximity to the woman he desired was too strong to allow his mind to dwell on anything other than her.

'Were you afraid?' Kiyoshi asked.

'Of what?' Kaoru replied. Kiyoshi felt her eyes upon him. In one way he was flattered that she looked at him, in another worried that she might not like what she saw.

'Of Barsolomew san, the ghost.'

'Yes I was terrified.'

'There is no need to be afraid,' Kiyoshi assured her. Kaoru fidgeted in her seat.

'Is he likely to appear again?' she asked.

'He sat in the very seat that you now occupy just before I arrived.'

Kaoru's stomach turned, not with the same muscular force as demonstrated by Kiyoshi's upon his first encounter with the spectral visitor, but with enough movement to make a gentle rumble at the thought of shared occupation with a departed soul.

'I wouldn't be surprised if he appears again. Please I assure you there is nothing to fear.'

Nakayama had hastily finished his evening meal, locked up the police station and taken a car from the police car park. He had kept in contact with Mifune via the police radio, and as Kiyoshi

Reconciliation

headed out of town towards Misaki Point, he was behind Mifune, who followed a couple of hundred yards behind Kiyoshi.

Kiyoshi realised he had been followed when the police siren wailed behind him. He felt sick and undecided as what to do.

Should he stop and give himself up or make a run for it in an effort to fulfil his plan? He was about four miles from his destination and decided to make a run for it. The police siren sounded disturbingly close and he stamped his foot hard down on the accelerator. The car surged forward.

'Hold tight!' he shouted. Kaoru glanced nervously over her shoulder, her face deathly pale. Kiyoshi could see she was disturbed.

'I'm sorry Kaoru, to have got you involved in this. As soon as we are out of sight of the police car I will stop and let you out.'

Kaoru trembled. Although it was already too late, they had been followed and would know Kaoru was involved, it would hardly be the proper thing to do to drop her in a dark remote spot on a cold and miserable night.

'In the back,' she gasped, the words hardly audible.

'Pardon?' Kiyoshi said, his eyes riveted to the road ahead his expression one of grim determination.

'In the back, there is someone sitting in the back.'

Kiyoshi flashed a quick glance over his shoulder.

'Barsolomew san!' he exclaimed. 'Why you appear to Kaoru?'

'Because she has already been acquainted with my person.'

Kiyoshi didn't understand why this made any difference but was pleased that Kaoru had further proof, if she needed it, of his sanity.

'Help me, police chasing.'

Bartholomew sat in the back reminiscent of an elderly aunt about to embark on an evening out with her nephew and niece.

Kiyoshi and the Grumpy Ghost

'Police are chasing,' Bartholomew corrected.

'Are chasing,' Kiyoshi hastily added, and thought this was hardly the time or place for a lesson in English grammar.

'Help me, if catch, I am in deep shit,' Kiyoshi blurted to use another expression he had heard the offspring of Masaguchi employ in class which seemed appropriate for this occasion. Bartholomew raised his eyebrows at Kiyoshi's expletive but chose to ignore it as he vanished from the back seat.

Nakayama was in front of Mifune's car, he had instructed his constable to allow him to pass, anxious that he should be the one to apprehend Kiyoshi. It was in his vehicle Bartholomew reappeared. He sat directly behind the large police officer, leaned over and removed the car keys from the ignition. Nakayama registered the removal of the keys with an expression of disbelief. The window wound down and the keys promptly vanished through the opening. The car began to lose speed and Mifune was puzzled by Nakayama's behaviour. His puzzlement turned to disbelief as he watched the vehicle veer off the road and slam into a tree.

The car, once the ignition keys removed, had no power although it travelled fast from the momentum. Nakayama turned the wheel in order to maintain a straight line and inadvertently activated the steering lock. The car no longer responded to the driver's frantic effort to maintain a course but obeyed the mechanical instruction to remain locked in one position and caused him to collide with the tree.

Mifune skidded to a halt alongside the car, leapt out and wrenched open the door twisted in the accident.

'Are you all right sir?'

Nakayama was stunned but otherwise unhurt. He sat vacantly as the weather made its way through the shattered windscreen.

'Are you O.K. sir?' Mifune reiterated.

Nakayama acknowledged the anxious face of the vertically challenged policeman and nodded.

Reconciliation

In the meantime, Kiyoshi had seen the shape of Nakayama's car diminish and take a bend several yards further on unaware of what had taken place. He continued to drive, his foot hard down on the accelerator. Kaoru sat beside him in total silence and struggled to come to terms with what she had witnessed. Kiyoshi glanced in the mirror for any sign of their pursuers.

'He must have done it!' Kiyoshi exclaimed.

Kaoru turned toward Kiyoshi and froze once more in terror. In her peripheral vision she could make out the shape of something sat in the back seat of the car. Something quite large, with a strong smell of musk.

Kiyoshi looked in the mirror there was no reflection of Bartholomew. Was he a vampire?

'I don't think you will be troubled further from those pursuing you,' Bartholomew boomed, and caused Kaoru to stiffen with terror.

Kiyoshi sensed her discomfort and placed his hand lightly on hers. She clutched it with both of hers in a grip of panic.

'It's all right, please don't be afraid,' Kiyoshi once again assured her.

'They not hurt I hope Barsolomew san.' Kiyoshi enquired anxiously.

'No they are in the rudest of health,' the hairy spook replied.

The car turned sharply around a bend in the road and illuminated a sign that indicated they had reached their destination. Kiyoshi pulled off the road.

The hairs on the back of Kaoru's neck still tingled when the automobile halted and under no circumstances could she force herself to turn around and face the passenger from the "other side". She hastily opened the door and stepped into the blackness of the night. Kiyoshi extinguished the headlights and turned off the ignition. The sound of the engine gave way to the crash of waves beneath the cliffs. It was a cold night and Kiyoshi drew his coat around him. He could just make out the silhouette of Kaoru in the darkness.

'Are you O.K?' he asked. 'Are you warm enough?'

Kaoru hurried around to his side and placed her arm through his; she was obviously unsettled by her encounter with the supernatural and sought comfort in the shape of Kiyoshi's arm. Kiyoshi on the other hand felt a sensation of warmth go through him that even the fiercest weather conditions couldn't have cooled.

Bartholomew's voice bellowed in his ear to remind him of the purpose of their visit.

'Sir, can we please make haste.'

Kiyoshi patted Kaoru's hand in a gesture of affection and acknowledged Bartholomew.

'Yes, let's do.' He took out the torch from his coat pocket and made his way to the rear of the car, Kaoru reluctant to release her hold on him.

'Have you got the Bible? Did I give it back?' Kiyoshi asked.

'Yes, it's in my bag,' she replied.

'Could I ask you to read the words? I think you would put more meaning into them than I?'

Kaoru hesitated.

'Please,' Kiyoshi begged.

'All right, but I've never done it before.'

'That's fine,' Kiyoshi said, relieved that Kaoru, if nothing else, had taken the first step to overcome her fear of Bartholomew.

'I think you're very brave,' Kiyoshi added.

'I think you are brave too,' Kaoru replied. The two of them took a moment to gaze into as much as they could see of each other's eyes until Bartholomew interrupted.

Reconciliation

'I apologise if I am interrupting something, but could we please get on with it.'

Kaoru physically jumped at the sudden interjection.

Kiyoshi smiled.

'Don't worry, he's always doing that, you get used to it.'

Kaoru said nothing and stood back to allow Kiyoshi to open the boot of the car.

'Here let me,' she said, took the torch from his hand and shone it in the appropriate direction. She was still reluctant to look at Bartholomew but eventually plucked up enough courage to steal a quick glance. Bartholomew looked back at her and winked. She quickly looked away.

Kiyoshi withdrew the bones from the boot and proceeded to make his way to the edge of the cliff. He placed them on the ground and tentatively peered into the blackness below. The clouds parted and the reflection from the new moon glimmered on the sea below.

'This should be O.K.,' Kiyoshi stated with the casual air of someone decided on a venue for a landscape painting.

He placed the remains closer to the edge of the cliff.

'Kaoru san, the bible please.'

Kaoru handed the torch to Kiyoshi who handed it to Bartholomew.

'Can you hold this for a moment?'

Bartholomew took the torch and shone it in the direction of Kaoru to enable her to find the appropriate passage.

'Thank you, I have it,' she said, and realised whom she had addressed.

'Ready Barsolomew san?' Kiyoshi asked. Bartholomew straightened up and handed the torch back to Kaoru.

'I am ready,' he replied, his voice firm with resolve.

'Can you see alright Kaoru san?' Kiyoshi asked.

Kaoru nodded, 'Yes.'

'Then please begin.'

Kaoru was about to read when another sound above that of wind and sea reached the ears of the trio. A police siren.

'Shit,' Kiyoshi muttered in Japanese.

'Quickly Kaoru hurry. We haven't much time.'

Kaoru began, Kiyoshi held the book whilst Bartholomew stood to attention, a look of great solemnity beneath his beard.

By the time Kaoru had reached the end of the service, the occupants of the police car had located them and were, as she uttered the last word, a few yards away.

'Don't move!' Nakayama shouted across the space between them.

A torch flashed and provided more light on the couple on the cliffs.

'You're under arrest, both of you!' Nakayama barked, satisfaction written all over his face.

'Mifune put the cuffs on Hirota san.'

Kiyoshi knew that there was nothing he could do to prevent his arrest but was determined to complete the task that he'd set out to accomplish. With one deft movement he stooped down, grabbed the skeleton and heaved it over the cliff into the depths below. Mifune rushed to prevent him but was too late. The bundle plummeted into the sea and made an inaudible splash before it sank into oblivion. Nakayama was furious.

> 'You'll pay for that; destroying state property, causing an accident on the highway, failing to stop, break and entering, misusing police equipment, resisting arrest, and I'm sure many more if I chose to sit down and think about it. Take him away Mifune before I lose my temper and throw him off the cliff after that, I presume, bloody skeleton.'

Reconciliation

Mifune rather apologetically took Kiyoshi's arms, placed the handcuffs around each wrist and locked them securely.

'This way Hirota san and you too please miss.'

Kaoru followed Kiyoshi behind the beam of light from Mifune's torch.

Mifune stopped in his tracks and his mouth fell open in amazement. Nakayama wheeled around to see what had taken Mifune's attention. He stared in disbelief unable to comprehend what he saw.

Before them was the figure of a man bathed in a soft white light. It was Bartholomew but not the Bartholomew of a few moments ago, but a resplendent Bartholomew decked out in all the finery of the uniform of a British Naval captain.

The figure spoke in fluent Japanese.

'I command you sir, to release that man immediately.'

Nakayama and Mifune were both rooted to the ground with sheer terror neither of them able to speak or run.

'If you charge these good people or in any way cause them discomfort I shall haunt you for the rest of your days. Do you understand?'

Nakayama was still speechless.

'Well?' Bartholomew boomed his voice drowned out the sound of the sea below.

'Y-y-yes...' Nakayama stammered before he shrieked at the top of his voice and rushed back to the car. Mifune quickly unlocked the cuffs and raced after his superior officer.

Kiyoshi heard the engine burst into life and with a screech of tyres take off down the road. Kiyoshi smiled at the English officer before him and bowed low.

'Smart, Barsolomew san, very smart.'

'Thank you,' Bartholomew replied in Japanese.

Kiyoshi and the Grumpy Ghost

'You can speak Japanese. How come?' Kiyoshi asked.

'I can speak any language now thanks to you.'

'It worked,' Kiyoshi exclaimed genuinely pleased for his ethereal colleague.

Even Kaoru had lost her fear, Bartholomew's appearance changed dramatically from a scruffy unsavoury individual into a sophisticated Naval officer. She was pleased for him.

'I have returned briefly to thank you and give you something in return for your assistance,' Bartholomew continued.

'Three things. One, you are an English teacher and if you will forgive me saying so, your English is not as good as it should be. Bartholomew stretched out his hand. Kiyoshi took it. The light emanating from Bartholomew's body grew in brightness and Kiyoshi felt a tingle run up his arm. I am giving you my vocabulary and all my memories and forthwith you will speak the language as a native.

Two, you will also have a first-hand knowledge of British History of my century.

Three, if you look in your coat pocket you will find a map. On the place marked is the treasure that I was slain for, merely a few yards from where my body was interred. Do with it as you wish.'

Kiyoshi felt in his coat pocket. His hand came in contact with a piece of paper not there before.

'Finally, have a good life together. May good fortune smile on you and your children.'

Kaoru and Kiyoshi exchanged embarrassed glances.

The school teacher felt saddened by Bartholomew's departure. All the frustration and aggravation, all the heartache and problems suddenly seemed worth it. Not because he had received a reward but to see Bartholomew for the first time as he was in his prime, a proud warrior of the sea.

Reconciliation

Kiyoshi took Kaoru's hand. Despite the regret of his tormentor's departure he had never felt so happy deep down in his soul.

Bartholomew faded from sight, a smile discernible on his clean-shaven face. Kiyoshi smiled back and gave a wave of farewell to his friend.

Kaoru and Kiyoshi stood silent in the darkness.

A beam of light shone upon them.

'Hirota san, can you give me a lift back to the police station please?'

It was Mifune, unable to catch his superior officer before he fled.

'Of course,' Kiyoshi replied, a twinge of disappointment not to be alone with Kaoru.

'I am really most impressed Hirota san, I think you must be very special person to have such experiences.' Mifune bowed low.

'I have seen tonight a most amazing thing, something that I never thought existed, a thing that has opened my eyes to a whole new aspect of life. I realise that I have been very narrow-minded, now, thanks to you and this most incredible event, I am a changed man.'

Kiyoshi felt awkward.

'Please don't mention it.' Secretly pleased, Mifune had said what he did in front of the girl he desperately wanted to impress.

'And now ladies and gentleman for the first time on British television it is my pleasure to introduce the well-known historian and authority on the supernatural, Mr Kiyoshi Hirota.'

The chat show host stood up and applauded Kiyoshi as he entered; the audience equally enthusiastic in their response. Kiyoshi bowed low and took a seat next to the previous guest.

Kiyoshi and the Grumpy Ghost

After the applause subsided, the host with a note of deference in his voice asked.

'Mr Hirota this is your first visit to our country. Tell me, the British Isles are reputed to be the most haunted country in the world, have you had any first hand experiences with Ghosts whilst you have been here?'

Kiyoshi, no longer the mundane harassed schoolteacher, but the well-dressed and manicured famous historian, cleared his throat.

'I have been asked to attend a country estate in Norfolk owned by her majesty the Queen to ascertain whether certain alleged paranormal phenomena are genuine and to shed some light on documents that have recently been discovered from the seventeenth century as to their authenticity.'

'I believe many years ago you donated some treasure that you uncovered to the Tokyo museum and that at the time it was believed you came by this through some paranormal intervention,' the host enquired.

Kiyoshi sat back in his chair. He could see the red light on the top of the camera closest to him. He turned to face it.

'Well sir that is indeed a question of great proportion worthy of an answer. It transpired a few years ago when I was a teacher of English in a small coastal town in my native country.'

Kaoru, seated in the audience with two children next to a frail Mrs. Hirota, reflected on those days as he began to speak. Kiyoshi's mother leaned toward her daughter-in-law.

'What's he talking about?'

'Barsolomew san.' Kaoru replied. 'Barsolomew san.'

Printed in Australia
AUHW010923130219
308592AU00006B/25